Welcome to

Hush

Check out the couple in Room 9006...

"Work with me during the day," Piper said, "and by night, I'll show you why Hush is going to succeed beyond my wildest dreams."

Trace frowned. "Are you suggesting—"

Her lips curved into a seductive smile. "This hotel is made for lovers," she said, her voice a husky whisper.

"We're not lovers."

"Anything is possible," she said, making him forget to breathe. "Everything."

Trace shifted in his chair. He was hard, as hard as he'd ever been as he glanced around the room, taking in the king-size bed, the toys and more.

"You think if we have sex, I'll have a change of heart."

She shook her head. "I didn't say a thing about having sex. I said we'd be lovers."

Blaze™

Dear Reader,

Oh, my goodness. You're holding a dream come true.

I had the initial idea for *Hush* several years ago, but that first glimmer wasn't half as exciting as the reality turned out to be. I got to work with five amazing authors: Isabel Sharpe, Alison Kent, Nancy Warren, Debbi Rawlins and Jill Shalvis. I think you'll agree it was the ultimate dream team. We had so much fun creating the incredible hotel that's at the heart of the DO NOT DISTURB miniseries. I don't know about you, but I want to stay at Hush and use *all* the facilities.

So let me be the first to send each of you a personal invitation. Please join us at Hush, check in to your penthouse suite. Dine at Amuse Bouche, have a massage, dance the night away at Exhibit A and play to your heart's content. Don't forget to peek into the bedside drawer for a naughty surprise!

Come visit us at http://www.hush-hotel.com. And don't forget to check out the excerpt at the end of my story from Isabel Sharpe's *Thrill Me,* the next book in DO NOT DISTURB.

Love,

Jo Leigh

Books by Jo Leigh

HARLEQUIN BLAZE

72—A DASH OF TEMPTATION
88—TRUTH OR DARE
122—ARM CANDY
134—THE ONE WHO GOT AWAY
165—A LICK AND A PROMISE

Hush

JO LEIGH

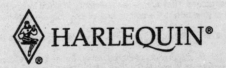

HARLEQUIN®

TORONTO • NEW YORK • LONDON
AMSTERDAM • PARIS • SYDNEY • HAMBURG
STOCKHOLM • ATHENS • TOKYO • MILAN • MADRID
PRAGUE • WARSAW • BUDAPEST • AUCKLAND

To all the wonderful women who built Hush:
Alison, Isabel, Nancy, Debbi, Jill and Birgit.
Thank you all...it's been a blast!

ISBN 0-373-79182-8

HUSH

www.eHarlequin.com

Printed in U.S.A.

Piper Blows It Again!

Piper Devon hit the party circuit in La La Land hard and fast this weekend with none other than that delicious bad boy **Alex Webster,** lead singer of chart-topper **FLAXON.** The two of them got so carried away, that they had to be carried away!!! The hotel dynasty millionheire$$ made such a wild and crazy scene at the Viper Room, she's been 86'd for good!
—Published June, 1996
National World Observer

Piper Goes to School!

Super heire$$ **Piper Devon** is registered in college!!! She's going to NYU for a degree in, what else, hotel management! Think daddy **Nicholas Devon** had anything to say about it? Wonder if she'll live in a dorm, instead of her huge penthouse suite at the ORPHEOUS? Will **Alex** sign up for music lessons???
—Published February, 1997
National World Observer

Piper's Trust Exposed!!!

Sources close to the heire$$ report that on her twenty-fifth birthday, Piper Devon received $50

million big ones!!! But there's a catch—in five years, she has to have made money on the trust money!!! Doesn't seem too difficult, but she also has to pass muster from stricter-than-strict Daddy Devon, who, we've heard, was not pleased with the idea that Piper was going to build her own hotel. If Daddy doesn't approve, she doesn't get the rest of her inheritance…over **HALF A BILLION $$$$!!!!**
—Published October, 2003
National World Observer

Piper's With Logan!!!

Piper Devon's new boytoy is none other than **LOGAN BARRISTER**, THE HOT HOT HOT lead singer from **WASTE!** The lovebirds were snapped in Rome, where they made the pigeons blush on the piazza!! Wonder if he's got his PIPER tattoo yet??????
—Published January, 2004
National World Observer

Piper's Sex Hotel!!!!

Heire$$ **Piper Devon's** new Manhattan boutique hotel is all about **SEX!!!** Construction began on the deluxe spa/hotel and those in the know say the theme is sex, sex and more sex! Private video cameras in every room! A lounge with exotic dancers! Massages (with extras?) 24/7! The name is HUSH, but there's no way she's keeping this a secret. What will her billionaire Daddy say about this???? Can't wait to hear....

—Published August, 2004

National World Observer

1

"Welcome to Hush."

Piper Devon gazed at the crowd of photographers and journalists gathered in front of her, here to get a preview of her spanking new boutique hotel. As she stood on a makeshift platform at the far end of the lobby, flashbulbs popped all around her, but she didn't even blink. She'd grown up in the glare of the paparazzi, and for the first time in forever she was able to use them for something she cared about. Her baby. Her hotel.

"Hey, Piper." She recognized one of the reporters from the *New York Post.* "Where's the sex?"

She laughed. Her photo-op laugh. "Keep your pants on, Josh." She leaned forward just a smidge, enough to give the front row a money shot. "At least until we get upstairs."

That got her exactly the response she was looking for. This time she needed the tabloids, needed them to spread the word that Hush was going to be the hottest ticket in town. That it was *the* place to stay in Manhattan.

One thing she'd learned in her years in the spotlight was that sex sells. Sex sells a lot. And she was the ideal spokeswoman.

"Does your father approve, Piper?"

She kept on smiling. "My father isn't exactly who I built this hotel for."

More laughter from the press. "Who did you build it for, Piper?"

She fluttered her eyelashes at the Channel 7 reporter. "For everyone who understands that Manhattan is for lovers. People who come to Hush want to explore their sexuality. Hopefully in the company of someone, well, close, but hey, there's plenty of fun to be had for the single adventurer."

"A vibrator in every room?"

"Better than a chicken in every pot, right, Elizabeth?"

The crowd of reporters laughed again. Good, excellent. "Okay, if you don't have a brochure yet, you can pick one up on your way to the elevator. We're going up to the twentieth floor, to the spa. And I promise, I won't get started without you."

Her staff, all in the Hush uniform of black tuxedos with pink ties, ushered the press to the four elevators.

She shivered with anticipation as the photographers clicked away. She'd dreamed this space, and it was now a reality. The glistening lacquered reservation desk with the same shiny surface on the back wall, broken only by the pink neon Art Deco HUSH signage, was perfection. The custom-designed furniture would have been at home in a grand salon of the 1920s. The artwork, vintage works by the likes of Erte and Bernard Villemot, was the pièce de résistance.

No one walking into this hotel would mistake it for

one of the Devon hotels. It wasn't like the Orpheus, her
father's flagship hotel and corporate headquarters,
which was opulent to the point of nausea. No, this was
a hotel for the young. The rich. The horny.

She stepped down from the podium, ready for the
next part of the tour. Janice Foster, the general manager
of the hotel, came up behind her, clapping her hands
with excitement. "They love it. Oh, God, this is so fabulous. I heard the reporter from *Vanity Fair* say he's
going to book himself a three-day weekend."

"What's not to love?" Piper said, taking Janice's arm
as they walked to the elevator. "By this time next week,
there won't be a soul older than ten who hasn't heard
of Hush."

"When are you going on *Leno?*"

"A week from Thursday."

"What do you think of putting together a basket of
the amenities for him?"

"Excellent idea. But then all your ideas are pretty
swell."

Janice laughed, lighting up her whole face. She was
young for a GM but she was damn good at her job. In
fact, Piper had stolen her from the Hard Rock hotel in
Vegas. Expensive, yes, but worth every penny. Janice
knew just how to pamper celebrities, and those were
going to be Hush's main draw. Of course, most of them
were going to be comped, at least initially, but the paying customers would flock to be within spitting distance of the anointed.

They caught the last ride up, and Piper took a minute to fluff her hair. She kind of liked this new short do. For years her hair had been long, straight and mostly blond. It was still blond, but a lighter shade, and it was spiky in all the right places.

"Let's just split the room down the middle," she said, turning to Janice. "You take the first batch through to the private rooms, and I'll head over to the mud bath."

Janice straightened her black skirt. She wasn't in a uniform, but she'd gone with the black-and-pink theme. Her dreamy Prada blouse was just sheer enough to show a hint of her black-lace bra underneath. "Got it."

The cab stopped and they were met by another salvo of flashbulbs and hot camera lights.

It took a few minutes to divide the group in half. Of course, she would have to take the other half of the press on this same path because, face it, she was the star attraction. She of the wild parties and rock-star lovers. She was the kind of celebrity America reveled in. She looked damn good in front of the cameras, so who cared if there was anything more to her?

It no longer bothered her, at least as far as the press was concerned. It would have been nice, however, if her father, and a few other people who should know better, could see beyond the facade. But screw it. They could kiss her photogenic behind for all she cared. Hush was going to be fabulous. A success no one could possibly ignore. And she'd done it all by her lonesome.

"How about you getting into that mud bath for us, Piper?"

She giggled. And didn't even roll her eyes. "Not tonight, Jack. But you call me in a couple of weeks, and I'll see what I can arrange."

"I'm gonna hold you to that."

"Now, Jack, I would have thought in a mud bath, you'd want to hold me to something else."

They were all nodding, thrilled with that juicy little soundbite. Didn't they get tired of it? She sure as hell did, but not tonight.

Tonight she was the epitome of Piper-ness. The flirty flake, the scandal in high heels. By Friday, her face would be on the cover of every tabloid in the U.S., and many in Europe. She'd made sure she would also be on some of the bigger magazines as well, including *Vanity Fair, GQ* and *InStyle*.

As they met once again in the spa lobby, Jason Newman, a stringer from *Rolling Stone,* called out, "Where's Logan?"

"Not here."

"Why not?"

"Logan's on the road. What's the matter, Jason, don't you read your own magazine?"

He gave her the finger, good-naturedly, of course. Hell, she'd known Jason for years, and he'd never failed to talk trash about her. "You two still an item?"

"We're still…something."

"Come on, Piper. Give."

"You're on my turf now, big guy. And tonight is about the hotel."

"Not fair."

"Yeah, well, life is like that sometimes. Now, you want to see the sex or not?"

A smattering of applause followed, and she congratulated herself on another bullet dodged. The truth was that she was incredibly over Logan Barrister, and if she never saw his smarmy face again, it would be too soon. *C'est la vie*. And he wasn't even the worst of her exes.

"We're going to the nineteenth floor, kiddies," she said as she led them back to the elevators. "Get your cameras ready."

"Where's the booze?"

She didn't have to see where that question came from. "Is that you, Ted?"

Everyone busted up. Ted Staple was from *The Daily News*. The man never passed an open bar he didn't love.

"You got it, gorgeous."

"We're all going to the bar as soon as the tour is done."

"Well, then let's get the damn show on the road," Ted said, and that was it for another few minutes. She could just stand here, smile for the cameras, revel in her joy.

It actually took about fifteen minutes to get everyone down to the nineteenth floor. She had prepared one of the largest penthouse suites for tonight's show. The Haiku Suite, designed by Zang Toi, was Asian luxury to die for.

Once everyone was in position, she started at the floor-to-ceiling windows and went from there. "In addition to the home theater experience with digitally delivered high-definition video on a flat panel LCD TV, including surround sound, we have one hundred television channels and ten high-definition channels that are private to the hotel."

"What do you show on those, Piper?"

She gave them her seductive smile. "The best erotica. Something for *every* taste. And if that's not enough…" She pointed to a black lacquer bookcase. "There's a personalized video selection prepared for every guest."

"How do you know what they'll want?"

"Questionnaires. Very specific questionnaires."

"Can we have some samples?"

"Of the videos? No. Of the questionnaires? Sure. The moment you book your reservation."

She moved to the bedroom. "These are handcrafted oriental rugs, and every piece of art in here is a museum-quality antique. So don't bump into anything, Ted."

She waited for the laughter. When the room was quiet again, she continued, "The walls are upholstered with silk, and the walk-in closet is paneled in sycamore."

"Yeah, yeah. Get back to the sex."

"All right, all right. Jeez." She went over to the low bedside table and opened the drawer. "Instead of the traditional reading material found in hotel drawers, we have thoughtfully provided a beautifully illustrated copy of the *Kama Sutra* and a selection of self-heating lubricating oils."

She walked over to the antique armoire, which she opened with a flourish. She could have heard a pin drop in the room. It was just as she'd predicted. When it comes to sex, no one's immune.

"This is the toy chest. Again, with something for everyone." She pulled out a long, intricately braided leather whip. "And if any one of you think you're going to print something trashing my hotel…" She flicked the whip against her leg, the crack loud despite the crowd, and tried not to wince. She'd had no idea it could hurt so much.

But she'd gotten her point across. It took a good half hour to go through the rest of the suite. The toys, the huge Jacuzzi tub, the erotic books, the selection of vibrators and costumes. But finally, it was time to go down to the bar.

Again, she and Janice waited for the last elevator. Unfortunately, they weren't alone, so she couldn't grill Janice for her critique. It would have to come later, but in her heart, Piper knew the preview had gone exceptionally well.

She let everyone get out in front of her, and saw the press had found the bar. So she lagged just a bit behind, giving herself a breather. There wouldn't be a chance for another one until the wee hours.

Just as her Manolo Blahnik strappy sandal hit the lobby carpet, she saw *him*.

Her heart kicked into fourth gear and her smile faltered. But just for a second. She should have known he'd show up. After all, he worked for her father, and who else would Nicholas Devon send to do his dirty work but Trace Winslow.

Dammit, why did just the sight of him make her tremble? She couldn't remember the last time they'd had a civil conversation. He couldn't hide his disdain, and she couldn't help but bait the prudish bastard. He just made it so easy. He'd never seen her for who she really was. And he never would.

"Hello, Piper."

She gave him her most dazzling grin. "Hey, Trace." She walked toward him, glad she'd worn this sexy little pink Versace number that made her boobs look huge. "I hope you're staying for a while. I'd like to give you the personal tour."

He looked her over, his gaze stalling at her chest on the way down and even longer on the way back up. "Actually, I am."

Her breath caught. "Excuse me?"

"I am staying. For the rest of the week. My luggage will be right in." He looked around the lobby as if he hadn't just hurled a huge land mine. "What, no bellmen?"

"The hotel isn't open yet."

He nodded. "No problem. I'll just leave my bags behind the desk until the tour is over. You do have room for one more, don't you?"

"Wait just a minute there, buddy. What do you mean you're staying here?"

"Just what I said."

"I don't remember inviting you."

"And yet, I knew in my heart you'd welcome me with open arms."

"Oh, please. With an open switchblade, maybe."

He came closer, all six foot two of polished grace, looking so smug she wanted to smack him. Of course, he pushed himself into her personal space. Near enough for her to smell the hint of his Platinum Egoiste cologne, feel the simmering contempt that was as ever present as his perfect haircuts. "I'm here to help you, Piper."

"Help me? Don't be absurd."

"It's true. I'm going to stay for the entire week, get to know the hotel, try to talk a little sense into you."

"As if anything you'd have to say would be in my best interest."

"You'd better believe it."

"And what? If you don't like what you see, you're going to tell on me? Cry to Daddy that I'm not being a good little Devon?"

"That's right."

"If I cared, I wouldn't have built the hotel."

He shrugged. "Have it your way. But I suggest you think this through."

She took a deep breath. It was important not to yell. Not to lose her cool. The press was here in droves, and she didn't want anything to deflect from the buzz she was working so hard to build for her hotel. "And why should I do that?"

"Because, my little spoiled heiress, if you don't, you're going to be cut off. Completely. From all those millions of Devon dollars."

2

PIPER STARED at him with her wide blue eyes, and God help him, Trace couldn't hold back his smile. He'd gotten to her. Oh, yeah. She'd never suspected that Daddy would pull the plug. Not Piper. She was entitled. To everything. So what if she was embarrassing her father, damaging the Devon name? If it felt good, she did it. If it put her face on the front page of the tabloids, she'd be there.

"What the hell are you talking about?" she asked, her voice a whole lot less cocky.

"I'm sure you heard me, sweetheart. Nicholas isn't pleased. And since he's the one who controls the money, he gets to vote with your inheritance."

"And he couldn't be bothered to come down here himself?"

"Trust me, you wouldn't have liked it if he had. I'm giving you a break, Piper."

"Some break." She took a step back. "Gee, Trace, what next? You gonna go tell the press? I'm sure they'd love the scoop."

"I actually wanted a chance to hear your spiel, but I

guess I'm too late. I think I'll go have a drink, though. Care to join me?"

"I'd rather eat worms. I need to promote my hotel. Do me a favor, Trace, find yourself some babe, and keep out of my way."

"Mighty snippy for a woman on the brink of poverty."

"I'm not kidding. I can't do this now."

"What about after?"

She headed for the reception desk and walked behind it. He followed at a more leisurely pace, letting himself get a feel for the lobby. It was nice. Very nice. Even Nicholas wouldn't know that it was a sex hotel from here. When he reached her at the desk, she was typing on a keyboard. She didn't look up.

"Piper?"

Trace glanced toward the bar, where an attractive redhead looked at him curiously.

"Give me a minute, Janice," Piper said, still not lifting her head.

"You got it." The redhead checked him out, smiled, then went back into the dark recesses of the bar. Maybe he would find himself someone to talk to.

On the other hand, it was so much fun to be with Piper. Especially when he had her at such a distinct disadvantage. People talk about the fun of tennis, but they didn't know what it was like to volley in the big leagues. Nobody gave it to him like Piper. Pity she was such a brat.

"Here," she said, slapping a key card on the black lacquer counter. "You can stay tonight. We'll talk tomorrow."

He slipped the key in his breast pocket. "You gonna give me turndown service?"

"Why should tonight be any different? I always turn you down."

He bowed his head slightly. "Touché. I really just handed that one to you. Sloppy, Trace, sloppy."

"Well, you just stand there and try to come up with something better."

Piper walked away and he couldn't help but admire the view. That little pink number hugged her in all the right places. No wonder the press loved her. She was stunning, and at twenty-seven, she was more beautiful than she'd ever been.

Not that it mattered. She was spoiled and reckless and she lived as if she were God's gift to the world. No concern for anyone else, no sense of propriety. She did what she liked, consequences be damned. Well, her free ride was about to end if she didn't make a real quick turnaround. He hoped, for her sake, she'd get the message. Piper wouldn't make an attractive pauper. She was awfully used to that silver spoon.

What the hell. He might as well check out the bar. He had the feeling he'd be seeing a lot of it in the next week.

PIPER FELT like she'd been kicked in the stomach. He wouldn't really... Not cut her off. It was a hotel, for heaven's sake. She wasn't selling herself in Times Square. She was doing what she'd been born to do. Sure, it was a new concept, nothing at all like the chain of Devon hotels, but wasn't that the point of a new generation?

The stipulations on her trust hadn't said a thing about propriety. Her job was to make money, and dammit, there was no way Hush wouldn't. He couldn't do this to her, that's all. She was his only daughter.

Kyle must have had something to do with this. Greedy little bastard of a brother. Always pandering to Nicholas. Damn him.

They'd both been born late in her father's life. Nicholas had met their mother, Alicia, just after he'd turned forty. Of course, he'd been married before, four times, but Alicia had been the one. How they'd wanted a son. Piper had been reminded of that enough times to make her sick, but Nicholas was from the old school. The very old school. Her mother had protected her from the worst of it, but Alicia hadn't been around long enough to help with Kyle. So her baby brother had grown up to be the perfect heir. She doubted Nicholas had ever once considered that Piper might be the logical choice to take over the company. Of course not. Darling Kyle would undoubtedly continue to live at Orpheus, continue to be everything Nicholas wanted him to be, and when it was his turn to ascend to the throne, he'd be just as much of a bastard as her father.

She walked into Erotique, the gorgeous bar, to the accompaniment of cameras, laughter, talking. People having a good time. She pasted on her best smile, and went into the fray. This was her specialty. Getting attention. Making the headlines. No one did it better than her, and dammit, neither Trace or his news was going to spoil things now.

She'd figure a way to get her father to accept Hush. She would. She wasn't a Devon for nothing.

THE REST of the night went on in a blur of interviews and champagne. Trace was never completely out of her sight. She'd turn, and there he'd be. Sipping the Cristal, talking to some hottie, laughing it up. And when his eyes met hers, he smiled. Smiled like he was on top of the world.

The prick.

What had she ever, ever seen in him? He was duplicitous, underhanded and a whole bunch of other evil things that if she hadn't had that last glass of champagne, she could think of.

Doing her a favor. Ha. He just wanted a front-row ticket. He couldn't wait to see her take a fall. "Well, you know what, Mr. High-and-Mighty Winslow? Screw you."

"What?"

Piper looked front. To the confused gaze of some guy from the *Enquirer.* "I'm sorry, what was your question?"

The guy, who was swaying just a little more than he should have, gave her a salacious grin. "So you tried out those toys in the cupboard upstairs?"

Piper kept smiling. "Not those, no."

His face fell but his next sip of champagne seemed to soften the blow.

"Would you excuse me?" She made a quick tour of Erotique; it was so beautiful it made her ache. Most of the press had congregated around the black circular bar, the pink overhead lighting flattering and sexy. She loved the high black bar chairs with the inverted triangle backs. She headed toward the ladies' room, running her hand over the only empty round-backed leather armchair, admiring the sea foam-green that matched the lobby carpet exactly. It was a killer bar, and it would be packed nightly. No doubt at all.

She nodded, grinned, waved like a damn parade-float princess all the way to the bathroom. She pushed the door open, saw the crowd, and made a hasty retreat. Hurrying as quickly as possible in her heels, she went through the lobby to the first elevator. No one came after her, and the moment she was inside the cab she hit the button for the spa floor and collapsed against the mirror.

She closed her eyes and let out a howl that while loud, was surprisingly unsatisfying. The elevator came to a stop and she went right for the bathroom.

The whole room smelled faintly of lavender. Peace, quiet and beauty surrounded her, a balm to her soul. She sat on one of the stools by the long pink marble sink, wishing she'd brought her bag. She needed to fix her lipstick.

Instead, she faced herself in the mirror. No photo-op smile, no tricks of the light. Just her. She had a problem, a big one. She knew Hush was going to make it, that it could be one of the hottest hotels in Manhattan. But she also wasn't a fool. She wanted her inheritance. Who wouldn't? It was one hell of a lot of money, and while it couldn't buy happiness, it could get her real close. Even though it would be a fine and dramatic gesture to tell her father to go jump in a lake, it would be strategically unsound.

The thing was, she didn't have enough time. She felt sure her father would eventually get over his problem with Hush. It would take a few years for Hush to be completely in the black, and she'd been counting on his help to get through until the cash flow was steady, but if he was going to be this stubborn... Damn, she only had a week. A week with Trace Winslow on her ass, which not only didn't help, it made things exponentially worse.

Trace knew exactly how to push every one of her buttons, and had no hesitation in doing so. He was a vile man, a hateful man. And good God, he turned her on like a light switch.

She dropped her head in her hands. This should have been a triumphant night, a glorious victory. She looked up again, met her eyes. It still was a victory. She'd make it work. She'd figure it out. But first, she'd go back to the bar and she wouldn't even glance at Trace.

HE WATCHED HER work the room, and even he had to admit she was doing one hell of a job. Gliding from one reporter to the next, she never missed a beat or an opportunity to make nice. Quite a change from her usual shenanigans.

How many times had he passed a newsstand to find Piper's photo plastered on the tabloids in some compromising position? Drunk or disheveled, hanging on some guy, at this party or that. The woman lived for notoriety. And here she was, playing the hostess, acting as if she were a responsible adult, when the whole world knew she was still a wild child. Who did she think she was fooling?

He thought about her latest in a long string of idiot men. Logan Barrister, for God's sake. His band might be at the top of the charts, but the guy had the brains of a trout. If anything he was more of a press slut than Piper. They'd been kicked out of more Manhattan bars than anyone else he could think of.

The tragedy was, Trace had a strong suspicion that Piper was bright. Really smart. If she hadn't been so busy trying to shock her father, she could have made something of herself. She knew the business inside and out. Hush had all the potential to be a first-class hotel, but no. She had to go and make it a haven for the kinky. It was a very expensive way to act out, and the consequences were far reaching. But would she listen to him?

He put his empty glass on the bar. He still had to take his luggage upstairs, get settled in his room. It was almost two, and the place had cleared out considerably, but there were still some die-hards left.

Piper looked as fresh as she had when he'd first walked in. How she'd managed that, he couldn't say. She must have been nervous as hell at this first sneak peek, but it didn't show.

He wouldn't bother her. Not tonight. Let her get some rest. She'd need it. So would he. Tomorrow was going to be…interesting.

PIPER WAS as exhausted as a person could be and still be upright. She made her way through the dwindling crowd looking for Janice.

There she was, standing by the leaded glass doors,

and oh, Mick, her hunky boyfriend, had finally made an appearance. Seeing them together, Piper smiled. They'd met here, at Hush. Janice had moved in a few weeks ago, when Piper herself had taken up residence. There had been so much to do to get the hotel ready for the opening date. And Mick, he'd been here, too. He was a master carpenter, and he'd worked on several of the penthouse suites. He and Janice had hit it off right away, even though she was eight years his senior. It looked like love to Piper.

At least someone was happy. That was a good thing. Her gaze swept the room but she didn't see Trace. He must have slipped out while she'd been busy. He was probably upstairs right now, slipping between the sheets.

She could've given him one of the penthouses, but she hadn't. He was in a regular suite, which was still incredibly wonderful, but he didn't have all the bells and whistles. Petty, but screw it. He didn't deserve a penthouse.

She, on the other hand, did. She had taken the Gaultier suite, and she'd kill to be up there right now. Only half an hour to go until she could shoo everyone out to the taxis on Madison. Till she could collapse. At least until 6:00 a.m. tomorrow.

THE SUITE was huge by Manhattan standards. It wasn't in the deco style of the hotel, instead it was Asian with shoji screens, a low California King bed with a deep scarlet comforter, Ikebana flower arrangements and Asian prints on the walls. There was an elegance in the materials that made Trace sigh as he put his suitcase on the bed.

As he unpacked, he noticed more details of the room. The sunken Jacuzzi bathtub with inset candles climbing the wall. The shower with three showerheads. The video camera and blank tapes standing in the corner of the bedroom. And then there was the selection of adult DVDs in the television armoire.

He had to laugh when he realized the book in the bedside drawer was the *Kama Sutra,* nestled next to a fur glove and a selection of flavored oils.

Not surprisingly, the bathroom cabinet housed a box of condoms and several varieties of lubricant. The whole suite was designed for decadence, built for two.

He walked over to the window by the desk and opened the drapes. There was the city, brilliant and shiny in front of him. What would his life have been like if he'd gone into family law, instead of joining his father's firm? As if he'd had a choice. He'd been brought up in the fold. The expectations had been there since birth. Probably since conception. On the plus side, he made lots of money. Lots and lots. Travel across the globe. All the prestige a man could want. Yet, here he was, babysitting.

The whole episode was a farce, a father-daughter drama with expensive toys. Piper wasn't going to change, God knows Nicholas wasn't going to budge. So what was the point? The hotel would be a sensation for a while, then the luster would fade and instead of booking the headliners, they'd get the wannabes from Jersey and honeymoon couples from Wisconsin.

If she was lucky, she wouldn't lose all her money. But

even if he was wrong and the place was the hottest ticket in New York history, Nicholas was still going to cut her off. He'd never met two more stubborn people.

The important thing to remember was that the outcome wasn't his problem. He'd do what he was paid to do, and let nothing else get in the way. Not his contempt for Nicholas's dictatorial ways, not his amazement at the circus that was Piper's life. Not even the way he got hard every time he looked at her.

He was a big boy. He wasn't controlled by his gonads, and hadn't been for a long time. That Piper could get to him like no one else was immaterial. Hell, she'd been a temptation forever.

They never spoke about that night. It had been her seventeenth birthday, and because she was Piper, she'd had too much to drink. The party had been at the Orpheus, and she'd asked him to come upstairs to her private suite. It been late, he'd had a bit too much champagne himself. He'd been totally unprepared for what happened.

She'd offered herself to him. Told him in no uncertain terms that she loved him, wanted him. It had taken every bit of willpower he had to walk away.

She'd never forgiven him.

But they still had to work together. It was ten years now, and still, the repercussions just kept on unfolding. Every meeting, every phone call, every social engagement where he watched the flash of her eyes, heard the silk of her laugh, he paid again.

He closed the drapes and headed for the bathroom. He needed to sleep.

PIPER FINALLY CRAWLED into bed at three-thirty. Bone tired, she figured she'd fall asleep as soon as her head hit the pillow.

She was wrong. At four, she was still thinking. Not about her father, not about losing all that money, but about Trace. About his being here for a week. A whole week. How in hell was she going to get through this?

3

MORNING HIT with a vengeance. Trace cursed the lack of room service, but blessed the coffeepot in the suite. He waited until seven to call Piper. He'd forgotten to get her room number, so he dialed her cell. She sounded more hungover than he felt.

"What do you want, Trace?"

"Breakfast would be good."

"Fine. When?"

"Half an hour?"

"Meet me in the employee cafeteria. It's on basement two."

"Fine." He hung up, then went to the desk and plugged in his laptop. He checked his e-mail, and answered most of it. His secretary, Terry, knew he'd be at the hotel for the week, and she'd cancelled or postponed his meetings. Because he worked exclusively for the Devon corporation as one of their attorneys, Nicholas had had no qualms about sending him down here, even though he had an apartment on the Upper East Side. While Trace felt a week was excessive, Devon disagreed, and since he signed the checks...

A week with Piper. Shit. It was going to be hard enough getting her to go along with her father's plans, but to have to eat with her, be near her. He should call Ellen. She was great. Smart. Pretty. A real-estate attorney he'd met six months ago. They'd gone out two, no, three times. He liked her. She had a great laugh.

He went to his briefcase to pull out his PalmPilot, but then it was time to go for breakfast. He ran his hand through his hair, and headed out.

Breakfast with Piper. Gee, how'd he get so lucky?

MEMORANDUM
To: Room Service and Housekeeping
From: Janice Foster, General Manager, HUSH Hotel
Date: Saturday
Re: Trace Winslow, suite 9006
Extra coffee!!! Check at noon and 3:00 to make sure he has enough.
Half and half in the fridge, replace daily!
New bottle of Stoli daily!!! Keep it in the fridge.
Fresh fruit and sparkling water at turndown!
VVVVVIP!!!!!!!!

PIPER SIPPED her coffee as she checked her watch. Trace was late.

There were only a few people in the cafeteria, but the number of employees was growing daily. Now that they were so close to the soft opening, they had to fill the ranks, finish training everyone from bellmen to house-keepers to dog sitters.

God, how many soft openings had she lived through in her life? It was the hardest time for a hotel. All the final bugs had to be ironed out, all the little things that only popped up after guests had checked in. Thankfully, the reviews wouldn't start for another month, after the official grand opening, but still. She wanted everything to be perfect.

Janice had been fabulous putting it all together, but most of the credit for staffing went to Lisa Scott, the head of human resources and Piper's oldest friend.

Lisa was the daughter of Jess Scott, who'd worked at the Orpheus for almost twenty years. Since they were the same age, Piper and Lisa had started hanging out when they were ten, and the friendship had continued. Deepened. Lisa and Piper's ex-nanny, Bridget Pollard, knew everything about Piper. They'd stuck with her during the good times and the bad, and Piper had no idea what she would have done without them.

Trace walked in, and Piper had to put down her cup. God, he was a good-looking man. It wasn't fair. He had a wicked body. Wide shoulders, slim hips, unbelievable abs. His hair was dark and thick, although it could have been longer. But it was his face that did the damage.

Perfect from his forehead to his chin. Expressive brown eyes that could communicate his every emotion or be a cold mirror. His nose was straight and fine, and his lips... He didn't have much of an upper lip, but what was there, worked. His lower lip was delectable, and when the man smiled, there wasn't a woman within shouting distance who didn't get wet.

Too bad he was such a prick.

"What do we do here?" he asked, standing in his dark gray suit, his pale blue tie, his body oozing sex appeal as if he expected her to drool or something.

"We eat."

He looked down at her cup of coffee. Her lack of food.

She sighed as she stood. "This way."

He followed her to the breakfast bar. There was everything from fresh bagels to omelets and waffles. The employees could come in here to eat, to relax on their breaks, to take staff meetings. At night, when the restaurant, Amuse Bouche, was open, the chef made sure the buffet was stocked with excellent fare.

She grabbed a tray and picked up some yogurt, fresh fruit salad and grapefruit juice. Trace got a waffle, scrambled eggs and melon.

They went back to her table, and for a few minutes, they concentrated on eating. Her gaze kept going to Trace's mouth, the way he chewed, his throat as he swallowed. But then he'd look at her, and she'd stare at her plate until she figured he wasn't looking. Then it would begin again, until she couldn't take it anymore. "So what's the deal? Why is Nicholas being such a jerk?"

"Nice way to talk about your father."

"I was being kind."

Trace frowned. "He's upset. You won't listen to him. What recourse does he have?"

"Disinheriting me seems like a radical choice."

"Oh? And what would you have him do?"

"Give me a chance. Give Hush a chance."

"Piper," he said, putting his fork down, "you've made the hotel into a bordello. You're still a Devon, and the man has worked his whole life to make that name mean something."

"It's not a bordello. Jesus, Trace, you've seen it yourself. I'm not ashamed about one thing at Hush. It's first-class, all the way. More so than most of the Devon chain."

"Its main selling point is vibrators."

She sighed. "I expect that from Kyle, not you. The main selling point of Hush is excitement. You and I both know that when couples come to Manhattan, that's what they're looking for. They want a rush, they want to feel cosmopolitan, exotic. I'm giving them everything they could ask for."

"Vibrators."

"Yes, and all the other wonderful things consenting adults like to play with. Look, all the boutique hotels have some kind of gimmick. The Muse has a dream maker on staff. The Library Hotel uses literature, including, I might add, erotica. Hotel Giraffe has the sweet-indulgence thing. Hush just does it better, with something more people want."

"You said it yourself, Piper. It's a gimmick. Gimmicks aren't what Devon hotels are about."

"No, they're not. They're about boredom. Look at the statistics, Trace. You know as well as I do that the average customer at any of the Devon hotels is fifty."

"Fine, you want to bring in a younger clientele, go for it. But not with sleaze."

"Sleaze?" She felt herself priming for a major attack, and reined her anger in. She couldn't stop the death grip she had on her fork, however. "There is nothing sleazy about this hotel."

"Excuse me?"

She stood up, afraid she was going to stab him. "I have meetings this morning. I have to go."

"I'll go with you."

"No."

"Piper, you're not going to get rid of me. I'm here for a week. Get used to it."

"Fine. We'll meet later."

"I'd like you to take me through. I want to see everything."

"I'm sure you do. I'll call you at noon."

"Fine."

"Fine." She grabbed her tray and headed for the exit, wondering what she'd done to deserve this…this nightmare. She knew he was watching her as she left, and she hoped he'd choke on his waffle.

TRACE WATCHED her walk away. Specifically that splendid rear end of hers. Today she'd worn slacks, black, that fit just right. A red silk blouse that curved over her breasts like a caress. And an attitude that made him want to…

He could do this. He was a professional. He dealt with some of the most cunning businessmen in the world. One young woman with personality issues wasn't going to undermine his purpose.

He'd make her see the light. Get her to accept her responsibilities. Or die trying.

PIPER HUNG UP the phone, then turned to her desk calendar. At three she had an interview with a new bartender. Her CPA was coming at four-fifteen. She wanted Trace to be in on that one. Let him get a load of the projections.

She'd already made dinner reservations for the two of them at Amuse Bouche, but that wasn't until nine, so if she could show him the hotel before her three o'clock, she'd have some time for herself after her last meeting.

She called down to the spa. "Caroline, can you fix me up with a massage at seven tonight?"

"Absolutely. What kind?"

"Whatever you think. I want to try them all."

"How long do you have?"

"An hour."

"Okay, you're all set."

"Thanks." Piper put the phone down. Caroline was a real find to run the spa. She had years of experience at the Red Door in Beverly Hills, and she was serious about making the Hush spa the best it could possibly be. They'd hired five masseuses, and the equipment, except for the steam room, was all installed and working.

In perhaps one of the best perks of her job, Piper was trying every technique, every masseuse. Just like she was going to try everything on the menu at Amuse, go into every suite and room. There was nothing she wouldn't do to insure that her hotel was perfect.

Not because her watcher was on the premises. Trace could go hang himself for all she cared. It was about pride. Making her own success.

Letting out a long slow breath, she picked up the phone again and dialed Trace's room. He answered gruffly, as if she'd interrupted something important.

"Are you ready?" she asked, keeping her tone neutral despite the fact that just his voice was enough to provoke all kinds of inappropriate responses.

"I'll be in the lobby in five minutes." He hung up, not bothering to say goodbye.

She put the phone back in the cradle, and dropped her head to her hand. Why did she let him get to her like this? Every time she saw him, her thoughts went directly to sex without passing Go or collecting two hundred dollars. It was downright Pavlovian, and worse, it made her feel like a fool.

She stood up, pushing back her chair. She would not think of sex with Trace, not in any context. Too many memories there, too much history. What she needed to remember was how he'd rejected her, how her heart had been crushed.

She turned off her computer and headed to the hallway. With every step, she took a deep breath, picturing herself confident, uncaring, cool as a cucumber. All she had to do was show Trace the hotel. Once he saw it for himself, he'd get it. He'd see that it wasn't sleazy in the least. Then he'd tell her father, and everything would be fine. It would.

She rode the elevator up to the lobby, and when the doors opened, there he was. He was staring at the painting at the end of the hallway, his hands in his pockets, the picture of debonair. She might hate him, but she couldn't deny that his particular combination of looks, style and chemistry was her Achilles' heel.

One last deep breath and she stepped to his side. "I thought we'd start at the top and work our way down." Without waiting for a response, she led him back to the elevator, and put her key card in the slot above the floor buttons. This particular card would give them access to the roof. She had another that would take her to the penthouse suites.

The doors closed and the only sound in the cab was the soft music playing from the speakers. It was Norah Jones, and Piper focused on the lyrics instead of the man standing so close to her. The long seconds ticked by accompanied by a solo guitar and the briefest hint of his cologne. She kept her expression neutral, her back straight, even when she saw the reflection of his eyes staring back at her.

She blinked first, looking at the elevator's progress as it went from the sixteenth floor to the seventeenth. Only a few more seconds and they'd be on the roof, and then it would be easier.

When they finally reached their destination, she held back a sigh, and simply led him outside. "This is the garden," she said. "Mostly flowers, but some vegetables that they use in the restaurant."

Trace took in the whole of the expanse in front of

him, surprised at the size of the garden and how lush it was with a riot of colorful blooms. It was beautiful and calming, with scattered benches and standing fountains.

He remembered this building. A prime piece of real estate, most of Piper's trust fund had gone to acquiring the space. It had been nondescript. A bunch of offices with a coffee shop and a dry cleaner, and something else he couldn't remember on the ground floor. There was nothing nondescript about it now.

"In the winter, this whole area becomes a greenhouse, so the guests can still come up here and get away from it all." She headed to her right, pointing out the retractable roof. "The pool, which I'll show you next, has the same kind of roof, which we can put up during undesirable weather. But during the summer and spring, we're going to keep it open."

He followed her down a short flight of stairs to the indoor pool, which was much longer than it was wide, Olympic-size, he thought. The floor was tiled gray and there were chrome sconces at wide intervals on the white walls. Next to the pool was a large Jacuzzi tub, and there were white lounge chairs and round tables lined up ready for bathers. On the far wall was a bar, not staffed at the moment, but it appeared to be fully stocked.

"Those are the locker rooms," Piper said, leading him toward two doors next to the bar. She walked ahead of him, sorting through some keys.

Trace let his gaze move down her body, captured by the sway of her hips. He preferred her in skirts, but this was a close second. He couldn't keep his eyes lowered, however, not with the temptation of that incredible behind right in front of him. Goddamn, it was enticing. It was nuts, how much he wanted her when he didn't even like her all that much. Yeah, she was fun, but so was golf.

He forced his head up, his thoughts away from temptation. He had no business thinking about her ass, or any other part of her. She was a job, that's all. Piper was enough trouble with her clothes on.

She opened the men's locker-room door, and he followed her into the small but efficient space. It reminded him of a lesser version of the changing room at his gym, fully equipped and ready to go. "Do you have a workout room?"

She nodded as she walked him past the showers. "It's on the fourth floor. I'll show it to you later."

"Great."

"The only thing left on the roof is the library," she said. "It's right through here."

She led him into a lushly decorated space that had the same domed, Plexiglas ceiling as the pool area. Only there was a coziness that took him by surprise. The wall that separated them from the lockers had a large fireplace in the center, and it looked to him as if it burned real wood. Looking up, he saw the chimney, which, oddly, seemed to fit with the other high-tech materials. There were cream-colored couches, each equipped with soft pillows, reading lamps and footstools. Rich carpeting covered the floor, and as the name implied, there were shelves of books throughout the room.

As he wandered, he spotted small groupings of chairs, coffee tables, chaise lounges, magazine racks. The bar at the pool was open in here, too, although there was a separation where the wall met.

"That's to keep out the noise," she said. "It's very quiet in here, and even though the sound system is wired throughout the entire roof, each space is divided to create the perfect environment."

Trace nodded. "So what? People come up here to screw during poetry readings?"

Piper's jaw tightened. "Yeah, that's it. We were just going to call it the Orgy Room, but we thought that might be a bit much." She walked quickly back to the elevator, and when they were both inside, she pushed the button to the nineteenth floor with more force than was necessary.

Trace relaxed, resting his shoulder against the steel of the cab. She'd faced front which gave him the chance to look at her, to note the tension in her shoulders. Even that expensive suit of hers couldn't hide her frustration. He liked her this way. On edge, on the defensive. He could control things better this way. When Piper was angry, she let things slip. Besides, there was nothing more satisfying than seeing that fire light up her eyes.

He wished he could see them now, even though he knew them as well as his own. They were a startling blue that most people thought were colored by contact lenses. Large, perceptive eyes with thick, dark lashes. Eyes that were made infinitely more beautiful when lit by passion or pain.

He'd been hypnotized by them more than once. Even when she couldn't find the right sharp words, her gaze could tease him to the brink of madness.

He wasn't about to get tangled up in blue eyes. Like those who'd been turned to stone by Medusa, he'd learned it was better not to look.

The elevator stopped, and he stepped into the cool hallway.

"These are the penthouse suites," Piper said, heading to the left.

"What are you charging?"

"Five thousand a night."

"And the lower suites?"

"Twenty-five hundred."

From what he knew about Manhattan hotels, she was in the right ballpark. It would be interesting to see what was behind the penthouse doors.

She didn't make him wait. She opened the door, stepping aside to let him enter. As he walked in, he caught a hint of her perfume. She still wore Samsara. Surprising. He'd thought that scent belonged in the past, along with her innocence.

He forced himself to focus on the room. The foyer was large, as large as some New York hotel rooms. The floor was Italian marble, the artwork on the walls Warhol originals.

"This is the Pop Room," Piper said, her heels clicking across the floor. "It's three-thousand square feet. There are two bedrooms, three baths, butler, secretarial and limo services. It was designed by Jean-Paul Gaultier. Our other penthouses were done by Stella McCartney, Donatella Versace, Zang Toi and Vivienne Westwood. The bridal suite was done by Vera Wang."

"That's a hell of a list."

"Good PR," she said. "They're all coming to the opening, as are their favorite clients. We're having several photo spreads done. The *GQ* will be out next week."

"So it's to be celebrities all the way?"

"They get the press."

"But they don't pay."

"Not in the beginning, but they will. They'll spend oodles of money here because every star worth his salt wants the world to think they're the hottest studs to walk the earth. It's going to be a badge of manliness to come to Hush. And where there are hot, hunky men, hot, horny women follow. It's as elemental as the tide."

"There's nothing here that these people can't get at any other hotel."

"Why don't you shove, uh, wait on that opinion until you've experienced the entire hotel."

"You think I haven't seen a vibrator before? Come on, Piper. I'm not convinced."

"Well, then why don't you just leave? Go back and tell Nicholas that I'm a very bad girl who doesn't deserve a penny."

"That would be way too easy," he said, his smirk so annoying she wanted to scream.

4

TRACE WALKED PAST her to the window and looked out at the view of the skyline. Impressive. He turned, scanning the space.

The color scheme was pastel, with sharp additions of crimson and black. He could see the attention to detail in everything from the crown molding to the silk drapes. Piper had clearly spared no expense here. It was the kind of penthouse designed to make the rich feel privileged, that catered to the most discriminating tastes. In fact, it reminded him of the Burj Al Arab hotel in Dubai—the only seven-star hotel in the world. Piper was aiming high.

"Let's see the rest." He stepped forward, but she headed away before he got too close. Which was good because his body thrummed with a need that was purely sexual.

It was insanity. His private hell. He wished he could forget about his job and just screw her through the mattress.

He followed her into the master bedroom. She'd walked over to the incredibly huge four-poster bed and her hand, with her long, narrow fingers, her perfect pink nail polish, rested on one of the plush pillows.

"We had the bed custom-made, along with all the linens. It's larger than a California King, and the sheets are six-hundred-count Egyptian cotton. Which, by the way, we've used on all the beds in the hotel."

"Not cheap."

"Worth it," she said, her hand skimming the detailed cherrywood headboard.

He wrestled his attention to other appointments. The velvet chaise, the deep burgundy walls, the modern crystal chandelier.

He heard a soft hum, and right in front of the chandelier, he watched a large slim screen lower from a hidden recess in the ceiling. Walking around to her side of the bed, he waited until the screen was in position. "Plasma?"

"The best there is," she said. She pointed to a panel on the sleek bedside table. "Everything in the suite can be controlled from here. The temperature, the drapes, the sound system, the TV." She pressed a button and the elegant draperies opened to reveal another floor-to-ceiling glass wall.

"So where's the sex?" he asked.

"Everywhere," she said, pointing him to a large armoire in the corner. "There are films, books, cameras, condoms of all kinds…." She swung the cabinet doors open. "Everything for the adventurous couple."

He could see that. Aside from the items she'd mentioned, there was another aspect of adventure well stocked. Silk scarves, fur-lined cuffs, a leather harness, riding crop. And that's all that was on immediate display.

"Of course," she said, "all really intimate accessories

are gifts from the hotel. Something to remember Hush by when the guests go home."

He struggled to keep his expression neutral. All he could think about were the cuffs, with Piper's wrists in them. The dark-red scarf covering those too-knowing eyes. Her body, stretched to its limit on that enormous bed.

Her hand moved from the cabinet door to the small of her throat. It was too easy to let his gaze move up those few inches to slightly parted lips, to the high color in her cheeks. To the hunger in her dangerous blue eyes.

PIPER CONTROLLED her breathing, but she couldn't stop her heart from slamming in her chest. She tried to turn away from the heat of Trace's gaze. She couldn't move. Not an inch. Because what she saw in his eyes made everything that had happened in the past ten years vanish.

He wanted her. No denial would ever be enough to convince her otherwise. She'd seen him like this before, and as before, her sanity fled and her imagination took over.

Images tumbled as the strange connection between them grew: his face contorting in a mask of passion as he came inside her, the feel of his lips as they tugged at her nipples. How he would teach her what it was to let go, which didn't make a damn bit of sense because the man was the epitome of stodgy.

Of course she'd had lovers after her embarrassing seduction fiasco with Trace. He might have turned her away, but others hadn't. Unfortunately, dream-lover Trace was far more interesting than her real lovers had been. Not that she'd never had fun. Heavens no. But there was always something missing. Something she'd made up in her weird little brain.

The smartest thing she could do would be to just throw the man on the bed, right now, this minute, rip off his pants and get it over with already. There wasn't a chance he could live up to the man she'd imagined. And then she could hate him in earnest.

He took a step. One step. That was enough. She broke free, turned her head, closed the armoire. Came back to her senses. "The bathroom is also designed for couples," she said, forcing herself to walk casually.

For a blessed minute he didn't join her, which gave her time to finish calming down.

"It's big."

She turned to Trace standing by the tub. "Big enough for four adults," she said, grateful to be on an even keel. "There's a separate sound system, a television, full access to lighting and an intercom." She pointed to the freestanding shower. "Six showerheads plus the water bar. It's also a steam room. The floor is heated from below, the towels are warmed to body temperature."

"What, no oiled towel boys?"

She smiled. "For you, honey? We'd make an exception."

"Oh, funny. You're a scream."

"You make me look good, lover."

"In your dreams."

She opened a mirrored cabinet which revealed shelves stocked with black-and-pink bottles. "We have signature scents, oils, soaps, lotions, shampoos. A small company in Brooklyn makes everything for us. Exclusively."

"You've thought of everything."

"Probably not. Yet."

He ran his hand across the marble of the double sinks. "Okay, I can't put this off any longer. Why? Why the sex angle? You must have known your father would never go for it."

At last. A conversation Piper was completely prepared for. "It's a niche that needed filling."

"Pardon the pun?" he said, his lips turning up at the corners.

"No, I don't think I can pardon that. I've done my homework, Trace. There's nothing like this in Manhattan. Nothing."

"Not even in Times Square?"

"I think your insistence in equating sex with sleaze is something you need to discuss with your therapist."

He laughed. "Right. I'm probably the only person in New York who thinks a hotel designed for sex is tawdry."

"No, you're just one of the sadly misinformed. This hotel is about pleasure. Consensual, mutual pleasure."

"The *Kama Sutra* in the bedside drawer? The cameras, the sex toys? Come on, Piper, don't tell me this whole place doesn't pander to the worst common denominator. You know damn well you're going to supply the tabloids with years of grist."

"And that's bad for business how?"

"It's not the way Devons do business."

"Devons make money. I'm going to make tons of it.

Just like always, it's the bottom line that makes my father happy, and you know that as well as I do."

Trace shook his head. "How can you be this naive? I could almost understand if this was Kyle's idea. Not that he'd be foolish enough to piss off Nicholas like this, but he's been known to make some bonehead moves."

"What?" She leaned back against the door. "A disparaging comment about my brother? I thought the two of you were thick as thieves."

"Kyle's a decent kid."

"Kyle's a suck-up of the first order. If Dad says jump, all he knows how to do is ask 'How high.'"

"He understands what's at stake. He listens to your father. He's not in the tabloids every other day."

"Oh, right. Kyle, the apple of Daddy's eye. You know what he told me? What he's going to do with his trust-fund money?"

"No. What is he going to do?"

"He's going to invest in Devon Industries. I mean, please."

"He's not dumb."

"Oh, wait. I forgot that everything's about money. Always and forever, amen."

"What are you doing this for, if not your inheritance?"

She shook her head. "You wouldn't understand."

"No?"

"Not a chance."

He stepped toward her. "Try me."

She headed out of the bathroom, not willing to play this game another minute. Trace had proved beyond any doubt exactly what mattered to him in life. The buck. And the only way he was going to get those bucks was by being a slavish toady to Nicholas Devon. The hell with who got hurt.

"I'll skip the suites," she said, feeling him behind her as she crossed the living room. She was cutting the tour short, but she had to get this over with. "Let's go down to the workout room, and then I'll take you to the spa."

"Fine."

"I made dinner reservations for nine," she said, closing the penthouse door behind her.

"Fine," he said again, sounding as frustrated as she felt. He walked ahead of her and called for the elevator. "I'd like to see the books."

"What, the one in your nightstand isn't enough?"

He gave her one of his patented glares. But just for a second. Then he turned away with a shake of his head.

The elevator door opened, and he held it for her. She passed him, careful not to get too close. She didn't want a repeat of what had happened in the penthouse bedroom.

What she needed here was a plan. Some way to get past all this defensive bullshit. She needed Trace as an ally, not a sparring partner. Unfortunately, she had a terrible tendency to speak before she thought when she was with Trace. Her reaction just came so naturally. Strike before she was struck. It had been like that since she was seventeen.

"You coming?"

He stood by the open elevator door. She'd been so

lost in her own thoughts she hadn't realized they were at the fourth floor already.

She nodded, then headed for the workout room. It was very well equipped. Six treadmills, four elliptical trainers, a complete free weight set, Nautilus machines and more. She'd hired two professional trainers, and was in the process of finding two more. "We made sure the equipment was top-notch, and that the trainers are highly qualified."

Trace wandered through the space. She wondered what he'd find to be critical about. She'd been to all the top hotels in the city and she knew this was one of the best facilities available. In fact, there was nothing second best at Hush.

"It looks good," he said.

"Gee, thanks."

He shook his head. "I don't know what you think I'm here for, but as I told you last night, I'm here to help."

"Right," she said. "Do you want to see the spa?"

"Yeah, sure. Why not?"

Again, they went to the elevator, riding back up to the spa level. It was huge, covering most of the floor, and Piper was incredibly proud of how it had turned out. Everything was designed to ease the most stressed of guests, from the colors on the walls to the very air they breathed. Of course there were the regular Swedish and Shiatsu massages, but there was also aromatherapy, sensual, sports and other massages that offered cleansing of the chakras, balms for the soul.

Naturally, she didn't broadcast her belief in such

things and would have shot herself before she admitted it to Trace, who would have ridiculed her mercilessly. But the truth was, she felt strongly about the body/mind/universe connection. Only, when she was around Trace she become completely disconnected.

"What's that smell?"

She looked at Trace who was sniffing the air, and she noticed the little furrow right between his eyes. A powerful urge hit to slowly run her tongue over that small patch of skin. She turned, cursing herself.

"Piper?"

"What?"

"The smell?"

"That's a mix of eucalyptus and chamomile. For relaxation." She breathed deep, putting the scent to the test as she turned back to face him.

"Ah." He faced the wall of cascading water that made up the right side of the reception area.

"The water recycles," she said. "It's tested daily for any impurities. You could drink it with no ill effects."

"Thanks, but I'll pass."

Caroline King walked into the room. She smiled at Piper, but when her gaze shifted to Trace, the smile changed. Piper had seen that reaction before. Trace was a very handsome man, but more than that, he had the kind of charisma that seemed to affect women in a very fundamental way. Fundamental, that was cute. The truth was, most women who saw Trace wanted to jump his bones.

Maybe there was a vaccine for that. She'd be first in line with her sleeve rolled up. Fact: the chemistry between them was undeniable. Now, how could she use it to her advantage?

"Piper has an appointment this evening," Caroline said, after she'd introduced herself to Trace. "Why don't you let me make one for you at the same time?"

"I'm sure Mr. Winslow has better things to do," Piper said.

Trace turned away from the reception desk and gave her a smile that made her teeth clench. "I understand there are couples' massages?"

"Oh," Caroline said, tearing her gaze from Trace to look at her boss. "Of course."

"That's true," Piper said, not at all ready to play this game. She needed time to think. To strategize. "They're for couples."

His smug smile said too much. "What other massages do you have?"

Caroline handed him the brochure they'd gotten from the printer only three days ago. While he looked at it, Caroline gave her a questioning look.

Piper answered with a small shake of the head. She wasn't about to go into her history with Trace with any of the staff, no matter how much she liked them. Only one person knew about Trace and that was Lisa. But even Lisa didn't know the whole truth.

"How about this sports massage?"

"It's wonderful," Caroline said. "If you have any specific areas that are giving you trouble, just tell your masseuse."

"Six o'clock?"

Caroline smiled. "We'll be ready for you."

Trace nodded, then turned back to Piper. "That should give us enough time to finish the tour and with the CPA."

"Thank you, Caroline. See you later." Looking at Trace, she said, "You can go through the rest of the spa when it's time for your appointment. I've got bartenders to interview before we can go over the accounting."

He nodded, walking with her into the hall. "What was all that about the couples' massage?"

"What?"

"Are we talking about breaking laws here? Is that why you didn't want to take one with me?"

"Don't be ridiculous. It's for lovers, okay? Not people you can barely tolerate."

"Dost thou protest too much?"

"You wish, you perv."

"Excuse me? Pot. Kettle?"

"Nothing in this hotel is illegal. Not at the pool, not in the gym and not in the spa."

"How can you be sure?"

"Because I'm not a madam."

"Then what's the problem if there's no line-crossing?"

She moved close to him, hating that she had to look up to meet his eyes. "Well, this explains a lot."

He raised his brow.

"Lovers, Trace, are two people who care about each other more than they care for themselves. You can look it up if you don't believe me."

He took a step closer to her, invading her space. But she'd be damned if she'd back away.

"And you'd know about that, how?" he said dryly. "Oh, that's right. Your latest rock-and-roll boy. I hear he has a really big…microphone."

Piper trembled as she clamped her hands to her sides. "Have all the massages you want. Do it with a poodle for all I care. Do whatever you want, I don't give a damn."

"You'd miss me if I were gone."

"Let's try it and find out, shall we?"

He laughed. "God, you are a piece of work. You can take the woman out of the tabloids, but you can't take the tabloids out of the woman."

"You really don't know the first thing about me, do you?" she asked. And then she turned on her heel and walked to the elevator. It was still open, and she pressed the button before he could join her. When the doors closed, she slumped against the wall. She wasn't going to survive it. Not for a week.

He was her poison, her worst nightmare, and he knew more about making her insane than anyone, including her father.

TRACE DIDN'T CALL the elevator back. He ran his hand through his hair, annoyed that he'd baited Piper like that. She drove him completely insane. Who did she think she was trying to kid?

He'd known her for too long to buy into this game she was playing. She might be able to fool the media, but there was no way Trace was buying into her act.

The hotel was a game, pure and simple. A way to stick it to Daddy. Just like the musician boyfriends, the drugs and the parties, the ridiculous spectacle she made of herself. He'd seen the pictures, seen her in front of the paparazzi. She could have been so much more. But she preferred the attention, the notoriety. She had the makings of an incredible woman, but she just couldn't break free from her image.

What he didn't understand was why he cared. Why he still felt compelled to needle her, to make her squirm. Shit. Bad imagery. Damn.

THE INTERVIEW for the new bartender had gone well, and once they checked out Shandi's references, she'd be a welcome addition. Just before four, Piper was in her office, going over the material the CPA would need for his meeting with Trace. She had no intention of staying.

Thankfully, her assistant, Angela, was so well informed that Piper wouldn't be missed. She could tell Angela was confused about her skipping the meeting, but it didn't matter. Piper had to get out, get away. There were a million things she could have done, but she wanted nothing to do with any of them. The second she could, she grabbed her bag and went down to the garage. She wasn't sure where she was going, just anywhere but here. Anywhere Trace wasn't.

Two limos were parked, ready to whisk her away. She could go to the Hamptons, Martha's Vineyard, the airport.

Of course, she'd have to be back at some point. Despite her desire to disappear, the hotel was so damn close to opening, she couldn't be away for long. Just thinking about all she had to do this week was enough to send her into a panic attack.

On the other hand, a panic attack would be better than what she was feeling now.

The valet stood at a respectful distance, sharp in his uniform, waiting attentively, but not obtrusively. Which was excellent, but it made her very aware that she was running away. That she'd let Trace get to her. Again.

She thought about going back inside, walking into the meeting as if nothing at all was wrong, but found herself wanting to head over to Fifth Avenue. Halfway to the limo, she heard something that stopped her. It wasn't a voice, but a sound. A rather pitiful meow that cut straight through her roiling craziness.

It was dark in the garage and it wasn't easy to discern the direction of the noise. A cat. A little one, she thought, but maybe it was just ill.

She hated that. Animals were her weakness, and although she donated a ton of money to shelters around the country, she still wanted to pick up every stray she saw. If she wasn't careful, she'd turn into one of those cat ladies whose houses smelled like a litter box.

So she had three cats. No biggie. Her place was really large, and there was always someone around to take care of them.

The kitty cried again, and Piper got a bead on it behind the Dumpsters. She inched her way closer to the sad, sad sound, her heart aching. "Here, baby. Don't be scared."

Tiptoeing carefully, she looked behind a pillar, and

almost didn't see it. Thank goodness for the flash of green eyes. The cat wasn't an infant, but it was young. And terribly dirty and so skinny Piper's breath caught.

When she reached down, the cat didn't try to run. She cried, but not with fear. Totally black, except for those emerald eyes, the cat curled into the crook of Piper's arm, and that was it.

Piper walked right back into the hotel, straight to the laundry. In two days there would be three shifts working here, but now, she had the facility to herself. She went to one of the oversize sinks. The kitty needed to be cleaned first, fed second. As she waited while the water warmed, she got her cell and called the restaurant.

"This is Piper. I need a can of tuna in the laundry room."

There was silence on the other end of the line. Then, "One moment, please."

She turned off the water, and then she recognized head chef Jacob Hill's voice. "Piper?"

She repeated her request.

"We don't have canned tuna."

"Oh. Do you have some fresh?"

"Uh, yes."

"Could you grind some please, and have someone bring it to the laundry?"

Silence again, and then an amused, "Of course."

It was there by the time the kitty was washed. Piper dried her with a towel, and the spiky-haired, damp cat attacked the tuna with a half purr, half growl.

For the first time that day, Piper felt at peace. Trace Winslow could go hang himself. She had someone to take care of now. Someone who'd love her, unconditionally. Who wouldn't turn away from her, who wouldn't break her heart. Who wouldn't make her ache from a need that could never be assuaged.

"You'll be Eartha Kitty," she whispered. "And you'll be mine."

5

LISA SCOTT shut her office door as the interviews for the day concluded. She was inordinately pleased with the staff they'd hired, sure that Hush would be the most perfect place to stay in the city. She'd lived in hotels her whole life, and this one was extraordinary.

She just wished things were going as well in her personal life. She had no date to the big party. Yeah, she'd be working, so it wasn't exactly a prime-date situation, but still. She was dateless. Had been dateless. Barely remembered dates at all. Maybe she could hire someone. An escort. Someone really hot who would follow her around like a puppy. Eww.

It wasn't fair. Every straight man in the free world wanted to go out with Piper, and Piper didn't want any of them. While none of the men in the free world gave her best friend a second look. At least not while Piper was in sight.

Perched on the edge of her desk, Lisa sighed. She should go outside the fold, meet people on her own. Take a class. Like Geocaching or oil painting.

In her copious free time. Right.

So she didn't have a date for the party. It didn't matter. It couldn't matter. And she wouldn't, no matter what, go to the restaurant and eat half a gallon of Chef's homemade ice cream.

A pint would have to do.

TRACE WALKED into the restaurant early, past the crush of well-dressed twenty- and thirtysomethings waiting for their names to come up. He knew Piper would show up at the last minute, and he wanted to form his own first impressions. It was an elegant room, but not overly so. Surprisingly, it was spacious, and the tables weren't packed in next to each other. In fact, there were painted partitions between the tables that made each grouping distinct and private.

The maitre d' was a beautiful long-legged beauty who he guessed was either a model or actress, maybe both. Just doing the restaurant gig by night, going on cattle calls and photo shoots during the day. It wasn't quite as bad as Hollywood, but at a hotel like Hush there were bound to be a lot of hopefuls.

She led him to a table in the back, separated by floral arrangements instead of partitions, and treated him to a stunning smile as she left him with the menu and a silent invitation.

He responded with a nod, then turned his attention to the menu. It only took him a minute to decide on the seared tuna. The hotel theme had carried to the restaurant, with black tablecloths and pink accessories and the deco prints on the wall. If the food matched the level of the decor, the restaurant would do well.

A waiter arrived and Trace ordered a Stoli on the rocks. A glance at his Rolex made him look at the entrance, and sure enough, there was Piper, on time to the second.

She smiled graciously as she headed his way. Of course, everyone in the restaurant stared. She was Piper Devon, the tabloid queen. She handled it like a pro. Smooth as silk, making everyone in her path feel special.

She'd changed from the pants suit she'd had on earlier. Now she wore a pale-green dress, short to show off those incredible legs, and if it were any lower cut, it would have been a belt.

Her smile dimmed as she neared the table. He stood. Even with her heels she was almost a head shorter. And so slender, he wondered, for about the hundredth time, what it would feel like to hold her. He'd have to be careful. Nah, Piper was many things but fragile wasn't one of them.

"Trace," she said, as he held her chair for her.

"It's a nice place," he said, moving back to his seat.

"Yes, it is. The food's wonderful. We've only been open two weeks and we're booked for six months."

He put his napkin back on his lap. "That's great."

"Speaking of great, how was your massage?"

"Excellent. Yours?"

"I'm a new woman."

"I doubt that."

The waiter came with his drink. Piper ordered a martini, the traditional kind, made with gin and two olives. When they were alone again, she touched the corner of her mouth with her finger, then leaned back in her chair. "What are you doing here, Trace?"

"I thought I'd eat."

"Don't be coy."

"Me? You know exactly what I'm doing here. I'm giving you a chance. A way to make this work."

"Do you agree with him?"

Trace nodded.

"Why?"

"Because gimmicks never last. The whole point of this exercise is to make a mark. An indelible mark. A respectable mark."

"And the only way to do that is to recreate my father's vision?"

"It's been proven. Devon hotels have stood the test of time."

"And so will Hush."

"I don't buy it," he said.

Piper's drink came, and they both ordered food. He waited for her to continue, anxious to know where she was heading with this. Despite what most of the world thought about her, Piper was no fool. She understood the game as well as anyone, so why the questions?

She made him wait. She sipped her martini, gave the room a slow once-over. When she finally faced him again, he recognized the determination in her eyes. "I have a proposition for you."

"Oh?"

"Work with me this week. You know what I'm facing. Be part of it. Everything. The last-minute cosmetic touches, the dry runs to get the staff comfortable, the party, all of it."

"And what, I'll feel like it's my hotel and use my influence to change your father's mind? Come on, Piper."

"I'm not finished."

"Sorry."

She leaned forward. His gaze dropped to her chest, to the soft, perfect beauty of her breasts. Dammit, how could she still do this to him? Make him ache with wanting her? Hadn't he earned immunity? How many years did it take?

"You work with me during the day," she said, "and by night, I'll show you why Hush is going to succeed beyond even my wildest dreams."

He forced himself to look up. "What?"

"Now who's being coy?"

"Are you suggesting…?"

Her lips curved into a seductive smile. "You need to make an informed decision. In order to do that, you need to understand what Hush is all about."

"Piper—"

"You were the one who made me think about it when you asked for a couples' massage. And you were right. This hotel is for lovers," she said, her voice a husky whisper.

She couldn't possibly…

"We're not lovers."

"And yet, if you hum a few bars…"

"Piper."

"Anything," she said, making him forget to breathe. "Everything."

He shifted in his chair. He was hard, as hard as he'd ever been, as he pictured the armoire in the penthouse, the toys, the handcuffs. He'd forbidden himself to seriously contemplate this…thing between them. Outside of his fantasies, at least. He could hardly admit to himself how often she came to him at night, when he was alone. Even when he wasn't. But in the morning, he always knew that Piper was off-limits. She was the daughter of his boss. More than that, she was completely wrong for him. In every way. She was wild parties, she specialized in excess and debauchery. She was Piper Devon, the woman he'd been hired to tame.

"Look, Trace. I know you don't find me unattractive. I mean, come on. The chemistry is there. We both know that," she said, her voice so low he could barely hear her. "Don't we?"

He swallowed. "I don't think I can talk about this."

"Tell me you don't think about it. About us."

"I don't."

"Look at my face instead of my breasts and say that."

He knew he was blushing. He hadn't done that in a while. But now that he thought about it, it occurred to him that the last time was because of Piper. She did have a way about her.

She leaned closer. "I've got one chance to catch the brass ring."

"Thanks. I like being compared to a carousel horse."

"You know what I mean."

"This is crazy. There's no way you're going to change my mind. Certainly not that way."

"I'm not asking you to betray your beliefs, Trace. But I deserve a fair evaluation, and you can't do that from the sidelines. Let me teach you about Hush. If you still don't believe in me, then fine. I'll let it go, and never bother you again."

He studied her. He knew everything about her face. The texture of her skin. The way her eyes became darker when she was angry. The tiny scar high on her right cheek. But he didn't understand this. She barely tolerated him. They'd been at each other's throats for years. And she had to know he couldn't be bought. Not with money, and not with her body. "You really believe it, don't you?"

She tilted her head slightly to the left.

"You think if we have sex, I'll have a change of heart."

She shook her head. "I didn't say a thing about having sex. I said we'd be lovers."

"And there's a difference?"

"Trace, don't."

"It's absurd. It can't happen."

"Are you sure?"

"Yeah."

"All right then. Give me one night."

"Pardon?"

"Tonight. I'm staying in the Pop Penthouse. Give me tonight, and we'll renegotiate in the morning. What do you have to lose?"

He chuckled. Saw the waiter coming with their food,

and schooled his expression into neutrality. He'd been hungry, eager to see the celebrity chef in action, and now he could barely spare a glance at his plate. He was too busy trying to figure out exactly what Piper was up to. This was as bizarre as anything he'd ever seen her do. But perhaps he'd underestimated her desperation.

She needed this hotel. More than her inheritance in fact. She needed what Hush represented. Her relationship with Nicholas was complex. She hated his methods but craved his approval. She flaunted her rebellion like a red flag, and reveled in his shock. He punished her with coldness. Yeah, she needed this. A successful Hush would be the ultimate screw-you to Daddy. The question was, did Trace want to dance in this twisted little tango?

Piper swiped her bottom lip with the tip of her tongue, and even though he knew exactly what she was doing, he still had to swallow hard and will his dick to settle the hell down.

"Will you?" she asked.

"Eat your salmon," he said, not willing to entertain her proposition. A week in Piper's bed. He'd have to be crazy. He picked up his fork and concentrated on the meal. At least he tried to. But he couldn't stop himself from watching her. She pulled every small bite off her fork with deliberation, using her teeth, not her lips. Perfect lips he'd imagined around his cock.

He swallowed, the tuna melting down his throat.

She sipped her martini, then trailed her finger over the rim of her glass. "Tell you what," she said. "I'll leave here after dinner. By myself. But I'll make sure you have a key to my room."

He didn't answer. He was too busy thinking of all the reasons this was a bad idea. And all the ways he'd like to take her.

"Did I mention that you can use anything you want from the armoire?"

Oh, shit. "You play dirty."

"I do a lot of things dirty."

"One night," he said, knowing he was every kind of fool.

Her reaction fascinated him. Equal parts triumph and fear. She was smart to be afraid. It was a dangerous game she was playing and the stakes were incredibly high.

PIPER WENT to her office, knowing she needed to cool her jets before she went up to the penthouse. It was crazy, what she was doing. She had no illusions about that. But it was her only hope. She needed this hotel. And, frankly, she'd grown too accustomed to money to adjust to none, which was shallow and selfish and all kinds of bad things, but also the truth. She'd never really gone up against her father on anything important. She'd learned the business, gone to school, gotten excellent grades. True, she'd also become notorious for her wild lifestyle, but in the long run, she was still Daddy's little girl. If she had more time, she would have had more options. As it was, her back was against the wall.

God, she missed her mom. She'd always been able

to talk to her. Her mother had been the intermediary, and she'd had Nicholas wrapped around her little finger. But that had ended when Piper was just a girl. She was on her own.

Trace truly was her last hope. During her massage tonight, the idea had come, and with it, frankly, some pretty interesting bodily reactions. But there'd also been something else. A feeling, no, not down there, a feeling that somewhere deep inside, Trace believed in her.

Okay, buried very, very deep. But through all the teasing, all the torment, there had always been a little glimmer. Hadn't there?

She went to her desk but she didn't sit. Instead she rested her hands on the back of her leather chair and looked at the architectural drawings on the wall. Her hotel, her baby. Once just in her imagination, now a reality, all because she wouldn't take no for an answer.

Trace wanted her. There was no doubt about that. All these years, and the two of them still couldn't sit in the same room and not think about sex. And once she had him in her bed, then maybe, just maybe, she could reach beyond those inflexible walls of his.

Somewhere inside him was the man who'd talked to a teenager about his own law firm, about becoming a different kind of lawyer, of actually using his talent to help people. Her future depended on finding that man again.

She'd had Angela bring her some things from home. Things she hadn't thought she'd need so close to the opening. They were already up in the penthouse. She'd brought the big guns: the red teddy, the black corset, her ridiculously high-heeled stilettos. If she was going to do this, she was going to do it right. No holds barred. She'd use every trick in her book, starting with the penthouse.

Tomorrow night, if he was still with her, she'd take him up to the roof, where they'd have exclusive use of the pool and spa. The night after, she'd arrange for that couples' massage. And then there was Exhibit A, the sofa bar, were she would take Trace to the final run-through before it opened to the public. But each night, they'd end up back at the penthouse. And each night, she'd take out another weapon in her arsenal. By the end of the week, one of them would break. She just prayed it wouldn't be her.

It was time to go. She had a lot to do to get ready. The elevator ride was the longest of her life.

The first thing she did in the penthouse was go to the bar and pour herself a cognac. With drink in hand, she went to the bedroom where she saw that Angela, as always, had come through with shining colors. Her lingerie was spread on the bed like a trousseau. She set aside the red teddy and the silk kimono, put away the rest. Then she ran herself a bath. Once the water was running, and the lavender oil was poured, she turned her attention to the stereo system. She would have preferred classical, but she chose something more seductive. Gato Barbieri. The *Last Tango in Paris* soundtrack. It was one of her favorites. She had no clue what kind of music Trace liked. Perhaps tonight she'd find out.

TRACE FLICKED off the TV and got up from the bed. He walked over to the desk, looked at his computer, but there was no way he was going to be able to work. Not when he couldn't stop thinking about Piper. She was up there now, waiting for him. Was she naked already? Or would she want him to do the honors?

His gaze shifted to the key card in its innocent white case. It had been there when he'd walked into the room. Shoved under the door like a ransom note.

There was no way he could justify going up there. So what if he wanted her? That was nothing new. What if Nicholas found out? It wasn't worth contemplating. To put his career at risk for sex? Not a chance. He had it made. Hell, people would kill for his life. So what if it wasn't his dream job? He'd stopped dreaming years ago. He'd smartened up. Done what everyone expected him to do. He'd gone to the right college, gotten the right grades in law school and moved into his father's firm and the rest of his life without so much as a whimper. It would be suicide to agree to Piper's plan even though he knew he'd never agree with her about Hush.

He walked to the window and stared out at the Manhattan skyline. The smart thing to do would be to get to bed. He could check out in the morning. He had enough information to write up his report without seeing another thing. He'd gone to see the housekeeping facilities this afternoon, seen the Exhibit A sofa bar, too, and while he didn't get the whole artistic-vision crap, he did understand what the sofas were meant for.

Piper was crazy. And so was her little plan. He still

couldn't believe she thought he could be bought. It would serve her right for him to do just as she asked. She wanted sex? He could give her that, in spades. After all, they'd been dancing around this for years. It wouldn't affect the outcome. She'd still lose if she didn't change her ways.

She'd end up working for Daddy in a Devon hotel. Her salary barely enough to keep her in her Prada and Kate Spade. Gone would be the burdens and opportunities that would come with her inheritance. Millions and millions of dollars. With that, she could do anything, be anything. He knew, without a doubt, that her father wanted her to use that money wisely. Only how could he believe that when she'd gone and built a hotel like Hush?

Piper believed that Nicholas Devon was a bastard. That he thought she was a fool. But Trace knew differently. Devon could be a royal pain in the ass, but he didn't do it out of spite. He wanted Piper to be more than she was. He wanted her to move from the tabloids to the financial pages. If she could prove herself now, the world would be her oyster. If.

PIPER STEPPED out of the tub and grabbed one of the warmed towels. She'd stayed too long in the water, and she had the pruned fingers to prove it. She'd hoped he'd find her there, but that hadn't come to pass. Just like the hope that she could build something of her very own. That she could win just one battle with her father. That she could stop wanting what she couldn't have. Who she couldn't have.

Well, she'd taken her shot. It was over now. Done and done. Her only option now was to stop struggling and give in. Rip the very heart out of Hush and turn it into another Devon hotel. Just like all the other hotels. She'd make money. Lots of it. And she'd wait. Even Nicholas couldn't live forever. Then she'd start again.

In the meantime…

She couldn't think of one damn thing to bolster her spirits. Not one. She'd gambled. Big time. And she'd come up short. Tomorrow, she'd begin the transformation. All she had to do was figure out how to approach the press. A meeting with her PR team was definitely in order. Hell, she might as well use Trace. He'd already figured out how to dismantle Hush. How to steal her dreams.

It was late and she was exhausted. She headed for the bedroom, not bothering with the teddy or the robe. She let her towel drop at the side of the bed, and then she slipped between the sheets.

It was almost midnight. Her heart ached with a sadness she could hardly bear. But she'd have to, wouldn't she? She'd have to put one foot in front of the other. Smile for the cameras. Take it on the chin.

Tomorrow she'd be strong. She would. But not tonight. Tonight was for goodbyes. For endings. For surrender.

She turned off the light and in the dark and the quiet, she let herself cry.

PIPER CAME AWAKE, her glance catching the clock on the table. It was late, almost two-thirty. Something was wrong. She knew she wasn't at home, it wasn't that. There had been a noise…something.

She turned and saw his shape next to the bed. A dark shadow within a shadow. Even though she couldn't see the details, she knew it was Trace. She felt him. Reacted to him with a speeding pulse and a tightness in her chest.

He didn't say a word. Just reached down, grabbed the edge of her covers and whipped them down, leaving her naked and exposed on the white sheets.

Then he was on the bed with her. She gasped as he grabbed her shoulders and pulled her up, his face so close she could feel his breath. His heat. His fingers gripped her tightly. "This is a bad idea."

She nodded. "Very…"

Then his lips came down on hers. And she was toast.

6

IT WAS PIPER. Piper's lips. Piper's body. Piper's bed.

But it was also good.

So good, he turned his head so he could feel more of her mouth, so he could tease her lips open, slip inside the wet heat and taste her. Moan as she tasted him back.

Her hand on his shoulder brought him up short and he had to pull away from the kiss. He reached to his side and turned on the light. It only made things worse. He could hardly believe how aroused he was. His erection was going to bust his slacks if he didn't do something about it soon.

"What's the matter?"

He gazed at Piper. Her face was flushed, her eyes wide, but what really got to him were her lips, the memory of her taste. He'd imagined it so many times, and yet he'd never imagined… "This won't change anything."

"Okay," she said, as her brows came down in confusion.

"I'm not going to change my mind."

"So you're here because…"

He sighed. "You deserve a chance."

She leaned past him and grabbed the silk comforter.

When she sat back she covered herself, and he could have kicked himself for starting this stupid dialogue. "If your mind is made up, then what kind of chance do I have?"

He opened his mouth, but he really hadn't thought this through. "Maybe I can be a little more open."

"Oh?"

Trace stood. He thought about leaving, but dismissed the idea when Piper caught her lower lip between her teeth. God, how he wanted her. But at what price? "I'm not sure."

"About?"

"What this means."

"What do you want it to mean?"

"You're not an easy person."

"You just noticed?"

He shook his head as he sat back on the bed. His hip touched her leg. Even with the comforter between them, it was an intimacy that erased all cogent thought.

"Trace?"

"What?"

"Let's see," Piper said, a sly grin changing her expression yet again. "You don't know what this means, and I'm not an easy person."

"Uh, right."

"And you were going to tell me what you want this to mean."

"I don't know. All I'm sure about is that I don't want to leave."

Her lips parted slightly as if he'd surprised her. Which was something, because he never surprised

Piper. On the other hand, she surprised him on a regular basis. "You don't?" she asked.

He shook his head.

"Why not?"

"You've been around reporters too long."

"That's an understatement, but don't change the subject." She leaned forward, rested her hand on top of his. "What do you want, Trace?"

He looked at her slim fingers, her delicate nails. Then his gaze traveled up her bare arm, the curve of her shoulders. The hollow at the base of her neck pulled him, and he was helpless to do anything but kiss that very spot.

Her head went back and when she moaned, he felt a soft vibration. He kissed up her throat, amazed at the silky texture, the scent of flowers.

She touched the sides of his face and when he looked up, she seemed as confused as he was, and as needy. The next kiss was on her lips. And then there was nothing confusing at all.

Piper felt the covers slip down, baring her breasts, and all she wanted was for Trace to be closer, to touch her. She pulled back. "Clothes," she said, her voice hardly recognizable.

He seemed perplexed. "Clothes?"

"Too many." She went for his top button as he smiled.

"Yeah." He started with his belt and by the time she'd finished with his shirt, his pants were unzipped. He stood and got naked really, really fast, which was good, because she needed him next to her, touching her all over.

She threw the covers off once more, and he laid down

beside her, pulling her into his arms. His leg went over her thighs as they picked up where they'd left off. Only this time there were all these competing sensations from the rest of her. Breasts against hard chest, belly getting to know the shape of his erection, the feel of his back as her hands roamed.

His mouth was ravenous. Teeth, tongue, lips, all of them couldn't seem to get enough of her, and it was incredible because he knew exactly how to kiss. Not with that huge open maw that made her feel as if she were drowning, and not stingy at all, but deep and erotic, telling her exquisitely how much he wanted her.

What shocked her even more was how much she wanted him.

There'd always been something between them. Way more than the adolescent fantasies she'd had, this was much more complicated. Although it didn't feel complicated right now. It was all about his tongue, his hand cupping her breast, the way he moaned when he rubbed against her.

He moved back, and for a moment they just stared at each other, both of them breathing so hard it was as if they'd just run a mile. The way he looked at her made her laugh.

"You look stunned."

"I am."

She slipped her hand down his stomach until her fingers skimmed over his erection. "And yet I'm sensing it's not too unpleasant."

It was his turn to laugh, and oh, God, it was a revelation. She realized she'd never seen him like this. Relaxed. Not scheming at all, and there was something about his eyes. Damn. He looked at her with pleasure. With joy.

She'd seen him hungry for her. Seen him suspicious, disgusted, confused. But never this. He'd never been more attractive, and she wanted him now.

She curled her hand around his hard length, and took fierce pleasure in his low growl.

"I'm praying hard you have a condom within reaching distance," he said, just before he leaned over and captured her earlobe between his teeth.

She shivered, and to her embarrassment, squealed a little. "In the bathroom."

"That's very far."

"I know."

"But worth it."

"I know that, too."

He sighed, sending warm air into her ear, then he kissed her hard. A second later, he was on his feet, making his way quickly into the bathroom.

She stretched out on the bed, not letting herself think about anything but the moment. Not the hotel, lord knows not her father. Not anything but the fact that after all these years, they were actually going to…

"Any preference?"

She turned to the bathroom. Trace, the man who wouldn't leave the house without his Armani suit, Bruno Magli shoes and silk tie, was standing in the light, holding up a fan of small packets, proclaiming his excitement impressively. She held back her giggle as she shook her head.

He hurried back, bobbing all the way. He dropped a pile of packets on the bedside table, then climbed into bed.

"Great expectations?" she asked.

"Hopeless optimism."

"Why Trace, this is a whole new side to you. I had no idea you had a sense of humor."

"Careful there, Piper."

"Oh?" she said, taking hold of his penis again. "And what are you going to do about it?"

His eyes went quite wide. "Nothing. Not a thing. Have I mentioned how much I like your hair?"

"Nope."

"Well, I like it short," he said, moving a little closer. His hand went south, between her legs, where he teased the tiny bit of hair she had left from her Brazilian wax.

"Cute," she said.

"May I ask you something?"

She nodded.

"Why is it we're chatting when we could be doing so many other things with our mouths?"

"I have no idea."

"Well," he whispered, moving closer and closer. "Let's see what we can do about that."

She closed her eyes when his lips touched hers. His fingers rubbed along the crease of her lips, the smooth skin incredibly sensitive. She returned the favor by stroking him, loving the feel of his thick heat.

As his tongue did all kinds of delicious things, he

slipped inside her, just stroking, up and down, teasing her with his patience. She ran her thumb over the head of his cock, spreading the slick around and down.

He evidently liked that, if his hip buck was any indication. She smiled around his tongue.

He liked that, too.

She gasped as two fingers plunged inside her, pumping fast. She arched her back, her body thrusting against him.

Just as it was getting really interesting, Trace pulled out and away. His hands went to her shoulders and he pushed her down so she was lying flat on the incredibly silky sheets. Towering above her, he made a show of ripping open the condom with his teeth, then rolling it on. Then he threw his leg over her hips, straddling her. One more kiss, a quick one, and he shimmied down, tasting, licking, nipping as he went lower. He spent some quality time with each of her breasts, paying special attention to her very sensitive nipples.

She got to know the texture of his hair as she encouraged him. Loudly.

He kept right on moving down. She hadn't known the pleasure of the light scraping of teeth across the skin of her tummy, the lick of a tongue in her belly button.

He spread her legs, nestled between them.

Piper's hands were still in his hair, and when he licked her, she yanked a little hard. "Sorry," she said, even though she wasn't. She wanted him to keep on doing what he was doing, only harder.

He was a very quick study.

Trace zeroed in, paying attention to the way she moved, how she responded. She liked it direct, pointed tongue, no messing around. Well, he could do that.

He loved to do that.

Her legs went around the back of his head as her hands kept him steady. She writhed beneath him, cried out, pulled his hair. And then she stiffened. Her voice got higher and more desperate, and he knew the minute she climaxed.

Before she even relaxed her muscles, he was up on his knees, his hands under her thighs, lifting, and then he thrust inside her.

He'd died and gone to heaven. She was tight and hot, and he didn't close his eyes. He just watched her, this amazing creature, as her head thrashed on the pillow, her mouth open in a scream that was low and throaty and everything he'd wanted from her.

He'd dreamed this. Her breasts, so beautiful, moved as he pumped into her, the rest of her pale, trembling, shimmering in the light.

She reached her hands up above her, grabbing on to the scrolled headboard, steadying herself, pushing against his every thrust.

His whole body felt on fire, all of it centered in the heat of this woman. This incredible creature who'd tormented him for so long. Their teasing had always had an under-current; lightly veiled innuendoes, unsubtle looks.

And now he was with her, in her, and he didn't give a damn about anything but this. He could feel it starting, the tightening, the pressure building, unbearably good.

He couldn't help it, his eyes closed as his head went back, and then he was coming. White sparks behind his lids, a roar of triumph from his solar plexus, and every muscle, every sinew tight to breaking as he emptied and emptied, feeling her contract around him in the sweetest vise.

Piper gasped for breath, the air burning in her lungs, her whole body trembling. It was as if her orgasm had gone on forever, that every time he moved, he stroked her, kept her right there.

She watched his chest rise and fall, saw the sweat on his chest, on his arms. He was so gorgeous it made her hurt.

All the years she'd thought about him, about this, and it was never this fine.

Dangerous fine.

Because she wanted more.

TRACE WATCHED her sleep. He should be doing the same thing. It was late, or rather, early, and he had no business still being in her room, in her bed.

But he couldn't leave.

They'd both collapsed. He'd managed to clean himself up, but barely. When he'd laid down, she'd curled herself around him, her arms, her legs. Her head tucked in the crook of his neck.

Of everything that had happened, this was perhaps the biggest surprise. Her breath on his skin, the way she'd smiled at him before her eyes had shuttered closed.

He wasn't sure how he felt about it.

Not the sex. This. The sex had been incredibly right, and better than anything he'd ever imagined. But being intimate?

He laughed at himself, not missing the irony.

He was sleeping with Piper Devon. A dream and a nightmare, all wrapped up in one gorgeous package. So what now?

Did he take her up on her proposition? Did he partner with her, help her convince her father that Hush was a good idea? He hadn't promised her, in fact, he'd made it very clear that he wasn't going to budge.

The thing was, now that he'd been here, in this bed, how could he go back to that empty suite? Knowing she was so close, knowing that he could have her.

He closed his eyes. Just for a minute. He'd get up soon, go back to his room. He needed the distance. To think this through.

So damn much was on the line. His job. Her future. And right now, all he wanted to think about was her body, her taste, the way she moved. Everything else could wait. Shit, he really should get up. Dress.

In a second.

WHEN PIPER opened her eyes, the first thing she saw was Trace. She tried to figure out what time it was. Early. Maybe five, five-thirty.

He'd stayed.

Last night it hadn't occurred to her that he'd leave, but this morning it seemed very strange that he hadn't. What was also strange is that she'd fallen asleep at all.

She rarely slept well with a man in her bed. Logan hadn't minded in the least. She'd told him it was because he snored, but that wasn't it. She didn't like to cuddle, didn't want to share her mornings with someone who'd messed her bed. She'd never felt the need to.

Lisa had told her she acted more like a man than a woman, but she didn't think it was that. She was just independent, that's all. And besides, she'd never once fallen asleep with a guy, even when she was exhausted.

So why had she with Trace?

Maybe it was the release of so much tension. Or because she had so much on the line.

She'd just curled up around him as if he were her body pillow and boom, she'd been asleep. It made her very, very nervous.

Moving as slowly as she could, she lifted her head from his chest, uncurled her arm from around his waist and rolled to her side of the bed. She lay there, frozen, sure he'd wake up, but finally, she had to breathe.

He didn't move. Would he wake up if she actually got out of bed? Did she want to get out of bed?

Turning her head to the side, she stared at the man. He was exceptionally stunning. No way around that. Especially with his hair all messed up like that. Her fingers tingled, wanting to play there again. So smooth, so silky. Like petting a mink.

She closed her eyes, turned away. She couldn't possibly be feeling what she was feeling. She didn't want him again, not now. Their deal was for nights, not mornings. Besides, last night was probably it. He'd had his fun, and now he would go back to being Trace. The guy who worked for her father. Who thought Hush was a lousy idea, and that she was an idiot with good cheekbones.

The thing to do was just lie here. Pretend she was sleeping, wait for him to get up and leave. He'd want to be out of here, she felt sure of that. She'd see him soon enough. Later. At nine, she had a very unpleasant task. Unpleasant but necessary. After that, she had a meeting with the PR people. Trace wanted to go through the room-service area, see how she was organized.

Then there were more meetings with Lisa and Janice. And finally, they were both going to meet with the concierge team. They'd hired four, and they were all extraordinarily good at the job, but it was important that Hush establish a precedent. The signature of Hush was to make people happy and comfortable. Piper knew only too well how demanding high-end patrons could be.

No effort would be spared. Meticulous notes would be kept on every guest. They would want for nothing.

Trace shifted, and she froze. Held her breath. But he snuffled a bit, then nothing. Just sleep. She could wait it out. The bed was fabulous, the sheets orgasmic....

Oh, crap. Why didn't he just wake up?

7

PIPER WALKED into the lobby of the Orpheus Hotel and headed for the private elevator, nodding at the general manager, whom she despised, as she passed the front desk.

The Orpheus was her father's flagship hotel, and it was one of the most extraordinary hotels in the world. Opulent, expansive and so pretentious it made her teeth ache. When she'd designed Hush, she'd made sure that while her hotel was gorgeous and luxurious, it had nothing of the stuffy ambiance of Orpheus.

Even the elevator, with its gilded mirrors and chandelier made her want to moon the security cameras. She held back.

Nicholas wasn't expecting her, but she'd checked with his secretary and made sure he didn't have anything big to interrupt. Of course she knew she was on a fool's errand, but she couldn't afford not to try. Last night had shown her just how thin the ice was under her feet. She wished she understood what was going on with Trace. She'd gotten her wish—he'd awakened at six-fifteen, dressed in record time and beat feet. She'd feigned sleep, and they hadn't spoken. Time enough for that when she got back to Hush.

She got out of the elevator on the top floor. Her father's floor. Nothing up here but his suite and the corporate offices. And the best views of Central Park on the Upper West Side.

She walked down the hall, her heels sinking into the plush carpet. No longer noticing the paintings on the wall, all of them priceless originals, she did note the intoxicating scent of jasmine floating from the fresh flower displays spaced on marble pedestals throughout the hallway.

There was no expense spared at the Orpheus, which wasn't the case in her father's other hotels. The Devon hotels all looked fabulous, if one didn't look too carefully. But at the Orpheus the beauty was bone deep. Because he lived here.

She opened the door to his outer office, and was greeted by the professional smile of his longtime secretary, Marilyn. Not his assistant, executive or otherwise, even though she knew more about his life than he did. Nicholas had a secretary. And a butler and a chauffeur and a personal barber. He was of the old school—the incredibly wealthy and privileged old school.

"Ms. Devon. How nice to see you."

"Thanks, Marilyn. Is he free?"

The older woman nodded as she headed for the double doors leading to the inner sanctum. Her desk was massive but immaculate, as was the woman. Not massive, just perfectly put together. Not a hair out of place. She'd worked for Nicholas for almost twenty years, and Piper had never heard her raise her voice.

Marilyn tapped politely, then went inside, making sure she left no room for Piper to see a thing. But in a few seconds, she was back, holding the door wide for Piper to walk in.

Nicholas was behind his desk, a sleek antique that was worth more than most people's homes. It sat in the middle of a room that looked like something out of Versailles. He looked well, although not thrilled to see her. "Piper. I didn't expect you."

"I know, but I need to talk to you."

He raised one silver eyebrow. Elegantly. Of course everything about her father was elegant. His suits were all custom-tailored in Italy, his shoes handmade. "If this is about the hotel, you needn't bother."

She walked over to the wing chair in front of his desk and sat down. Her posture was perfect, her demeanor schooled as she'd been taught from infancy. "It is about the hotel."

"We've been over this."

"Yes, we have. But you haven't even come to see it."

"I've had my reports."

"I'm sure Trace told you everything you wanted to hear. But it's not the same. I think you'd be very surprised if you came down to see it. We're booked for months, with more reservations coming in every day. The restaurant has gotten incredible reviews, and the coverage is unprecedented. It can't fail."

Her father smiled. It wasn't a pleasant thing to see. "It can fail. You're pandering to the worst of human nature. Sex is fine for bordellos, not first-class hotels."

"There's nothing second-class about Hush."

"The very idea of it is déclassé. Tawdry."

"If you came to see it—"

"I won't be associated with the hotel as it stands. I don't know how I could be clearer about the situation."

"All I'm asking for is two years. If I can't make a go of it after that, fine. I'll make it a perfect little Devon hotel. But I won't need to. In two years, we'll be fully operational and well in the black."

"Piper—"

"I'm not even asking you to give me the money. Just loan it to me. You know better than anyone how much money it takes to launch a hotel, especially in Manhattan. I've used up most of the trust, but I know I'll earn it all back, plus a ton more. As soon as the cash flow improves, we can't help but make a profit. If I fail, which I won't, I'll pay back every cent. You can't lose."

"Of course I can. You're not just disgracing yourself with this folly. I have my reputation to think about."

"Your reputation? Are you joking?"

"I never joke about my hotels."

Piper took a deep breath. She shouldn't be angry. She'd known before she left this morning that he'd say exactly this. So why did she feel like throwing the fifteenth-century desk clock through the twenty-four carat gilded mirror?

"If that's all, I have phone calls to make."

She stood up. "That's all for now. But it's not over."

"Please, Piper. Don't embarrass yourself any further."

"You're not a young Turk anymore, Dad. And it isn't

the forties. It's time for new blood, new ideas. I read the financial news, and the Devon name doesn't mean what it used to."

The only response she got from her father was a short huff and a slight reddening of his cheeks. He picked up his phone and turned to stare out the window.

"You and Trace are perfect for each other. You've both turned being a bastard into an art form."

With his back to her he said, "You have four days to reconsider."

When she left, she didn't even slam the door behind her.

TRACE HAD just finished dressing after his shower when he heard the knock on the door, but instead of room service there was a small woman wearing a pink hat. In her arms was a black cat with a pink collar.

"May I help you?"

"You're Trace Winslow, right?"

He nodded.

"Piper said that you'd watch Eartha Kitty until she got back."

"Excuse me?"

She held out the cat, who looked at him with suspicious eyes. "Eartha Kitty. I have to go shopping and Piper didn't want to leave her alone because they're still working on the shelves and she was afraid that Eartha would get out or get hurt, so she told me to bring her up here until she got back."

"No."

The woman blinked. So did the cat. "Excuse me?"

"I'm not a cat sitter. You'll have to find someone else."

"But Piper said—"

"I don't work for Piper."

"Oh. Well, gee."

Trace was going to shut the door, but the woman looked so distraught that he hesitated.

"It's just for a couple of hours, and the kitty will just curl up and go to sleep. You'll never even notice that she's here."

"Dammit." He took the cat, holding it well away from his suit. Piper would owe him. Big time.

PIPER LEANED BACK in her chair as Lisa finished her phone call. They immediately resumed their conversation. "It's confusing the hell out of me," Piper said. She sipped at her black currant tea. Lisa would help. She knew Piper better than anyone on earth, and she wasn't afraid to tell the truth.

She'd been Piper's best friend forever, and the bond between them had strengthened immeasurably after Piper's mother's death just after Piper's eleventh birthday. Now that Lisa was the new head of human resources for the hotel, Piper couldn't be happier.

"What, exactly, did he say?" Lisa asked, folding her hands neatly on top of her desk.

"That he wasn't going to be swayed by any of this. That he had no intention of talking to my father."

Lisa shook her head as she gave Piper a pitying look. "So basically, you gave him a freebie and he's upstairs now gloating."

"Oh, God."

Lisa leaned forward. "Holy crap, you wanted him. You still do."

"I do not!"

"Liar. Your nose is growing as you sit there. Shit, how many years have you been telling me you hate Trace Winslow? And all this time, you've been wanting to get him in the sack."

"Cut it out, Lisa. I have not. I'm desperate here. Do you have any idea how much money we're talking about? I can't just turn my back on it."

"Right. It was a political maneuver. If Trace had been, say, four foot five and a hunchback, you would have offered him the same deal."

Sometimes she hated Lisa. The woman knew her far too well. "Whose side are you on?"

"Truth, justice and the American way."

Piper nearly spit her tea. She wiped her mouth with a tissue and put her cup down. "So fine. I'm a slut of the first order, and Trace has been my secret dream. The question now is what do I do?"

Lisa was Piper's opposite in so many ways. She was dark where Piper was fair; she was only five-four, and there was something distinctly exotic about her beauty, which, being a smart cookie, Lisa parlayed into a very unique and enviable style. Right now, though, her almond-shaped dark eyes were studying Piper in a disquieting manner.

"What?" she asked, suspicious now.

"Do you really think Trace could change his mind?"

"I don't know. I think so. Despite our rocky history, I have gotten to know him a little over the years, and he's not a total schmuck. Of all the people that work for Nicholas, he's the most sensible, and he's softened the old man in surprising ways. It would be huge to get him on my side. What I don't know is if he really thinks Hush is a mistake, or if he just thinks it's not Devon enough."

"Well, then, I guess you can't afford to alienate him."

"I never could afford to do that. I just wish I knew what he was thinking."

"Ask him."

"Lisa. Be serious."

"I am. The two of you love the battle so much, you don't even know how to talk to each other anymore. Of course, that could have all been about wanting to boff like bunnies."

Piper was going to object but her friend might be right. About the boffing part, at least.

"So what the hell do you have to lose? Talk to the man. Be honest with him. Stop playing games."

"Easy for you to say."

"I know. You establish these weird rules, and then it's hard to break them. But you've got bigger issues here than sparkling wit and double entendres. Go for it, babe. Give it your best shot."

Piper nodded. "I'd better go rescue him."

"From?"

"I had Ruth give him the cat while I was gone."

Lisa cracked up. She'd known Trace for years, too,

and knew his feelings about cats. "Oh, yeah. This is gonna be a fun week."

"Don't remind me. I'll see you later."

"Good luck."

She'd need it. She left Lisa's office and headed for the elevators, wondering just how bad it was going to be with Trace. And if her whole world was going to blow up in her face.

TRACE STARED into the intense green eyes before him. For the past two hours he'd been tormented by the unwavering gaze, but this was the last straw.

It was Piper's fault, of course. She'd known just what it would be like for him, had counted on it, he felt sure. And still, she'd stuck him in this nightmare.

He thought about leaving. Dammit, he had things to do. He'd wanted to finish going through his e-mail before Piper returned. But those eyes. They stared at him with such manipulative pleading.

"Go away," he said.

The cat didn't budge. She didn't care that she was shedding all over his laptop. That his suit was covered with tiny little hairs that wouldn't come out no matter how vigorously he used his clothes brush. Why Piper had instructed her "pet concierge" to bring him the damn cat was beyond his comprehension. Piper knew how he felt about cats. He liked them just fine, as long as they belonged to someone else and didn't bother him. He'd had to put up with Piper's pet nonsense far too often. This was just, pardon the pun, petulance on her part.

It wasn't his job, dammit, to watch the pets. Eartha Kitty. What the hell kind of name was that?

"Shoo," he said, pushing the little black behind.

The cat meowed, but didn't move.

Trace picked her up and put her on the carpet. Of course the last three times he'd done that, she'd scurried right back onto his desk and over to his computer. Before she could do it again, he lifted the laptop, shook it, releasing a shower of black hairs, then closed it tight. "Ha," he said.

The cat was unimpressed.

Where was Piper, anyway? They were supposed to meet with the publicity team in half an hour. He wasn't bringing the damn cat with him.

His cell rang, and he got it from his jacket. "Trace Winslow."

"Exactly what is going on?"

He recognized Nicholas Devon's voice immediately. The old man had just come back from London. He had a mistress there, a baroness. She wasn't his only one. Nicholas might be almost seventy, but he had the libido of a much younger man. Either that, or his women hoped to get something out of the will. Fat chance.

"Piper's going to fight it to the end," he said.

"So I gathered. She was here this morning. Wanting to make a deal."

Trace didn't think it wise to mention the deal Piper had made with him. "She's convinced Hush is going to make her a fortune. You know how stubborn she can be."

Nicholas grunted. "I was hoping you would be more persuasive than I've been."

"I will be. I'm going to be here—ow!"

"Trace?"

The damn cat was climbing his leg. And it had very sharp claws. "Nothing, sir, it's the cat."

"What cat?"

"Piper picked up another stray."

"I thought you were at the hotel."

"I am. And we're meeting with her publicity team shortly. I don't want to be late."

"Despite what Piper believes, I don't want to see her fail, Trace. I know I can depend on you."

"Yes, sir."

Nicholas hung up, and Trace turned off his cell. He moved the cat to the center of his lap. He had no illusions about what Nicholas wanted him to do. Use his past with Piper to influence her. He wondered what the old man would think if he found out that his influence was being exerted in his daughter's bed.

He still couldn't believe she was naive enough to think sleeping with her would change anything. The hotel was going to belong to Devon no matter what. Nicholas wouldn't have it any other way. The best thing Trace could do for Piper would be to give her an out. A chance to cover her losses before the papers turned her into a laughingstock. Before she lost everything.

He thought about last night. Shit, it had been amazing. The most thrilling night he could ever remember. Which meant that he couldn't possibly risk doing it again. He'd never been a man to put anything, let alone sex, before business, but when he'd been in her last night, he'd have signed away his life. Foolish and dangerous. He couldn't let her get too close, no matter what she did to him. Nicholas trusted him to straighten Piper out. Which is exactly what he would do.

There were a lot of things right about Hush, and she could even continue to have some of the X-rated extras, if she acted now. Which is what he intended to emphasize at the PR meeting. If Piper decided to return. And take this damn cat.

The feline in question had curled into a small black ball, which would have been a relief if she wasn't purring so loudly. How could something so tiny be so noisy? And messy?

He lifted the cat, trying hard not to get her riled up, and walked her over to the bed. She blinked up at him, lifting her head from the curve of her paws.

"Don't even start," he said.

The cat meowed.

"Uh-uh—" He pointed, giving her his don't-screw-with-me face.

Completely unfazed, the cat stretched, pushing her rump up in the air.

"I've known women like you," he said, "and it won't work on me. So either you sit down right now, or it's out in the hall."

Eartha blinked, turned her rump to his face and sat again.

"I can see why Piper likes you."

He headed for the bathroom to try and clean his jacket again, but a knock stopped him.

He opened the door, and was blindsided once more by Piper's beauty. She'd always affected him, but now it was like a physical blow. Jesus.

He forced himself to get his mind out of his pants. She was a beautiful woman. He'd always known that. She made it seem effortless, as if she'd dashed out of bed, thrown on the nearest designer duds and headed out the door. He knew that wasn't so. She'd learned from the best how to look that way. The finest hairdressers, experts in makeup and style. She was always ready for her close-up. Which made him wonder why she let those tabloids catch her at her worst.

"How is she?"

"Shedding," he said, pointing to the fur ball on the bed.

Piper brushed by him and scooped the cat into her arms. Thank goodness she wasn't one of those baby talkers. That would have been beyond the pale. As it was, she spoke to Eartha as if to a friend, something she'd never done with him.

"We're going to be late."

"I need to drop her off at the spa. I'll meet you in my office," she said, hardly looking his way.

Anger flooded his body, and he wasn't exactly sure why, except that it was Piper. He grabbed his briefcase, thought about his clothes brush, but dismissed it. Maybe he could talk to her PR people before she got there, convince them that there could be significant benefits to seeing his point of view.

They both reached the door at the same time, and her scent, subtle and sensuous, hit him hard. He stepped back and she gave him a small smile. Which turned into a larger smile as she continued to pet the cat.

"What?"

"Thank you."

"I had no choice."

"Of course you didn't."

He cleared his throat, moved away from her. "Don't fret, Piper. I'm still the same bastard I was yesterday."

He watched as the smile vanished, as the tenuous connection that had been there a second ago snapped apart. Which was the point of the comment. What he hadn't figured on was wanting to take it back.

8

MEMORANDUM
To: Staff
From: Janice Foster, General Manager, HUSH Hotel
Date: Sunday
Re: Pool
Ms. Devon will be entertaining in the pool area this evening. It will be OFF-LIMITS to all staff after 8:00 p.m. Please have all food, wine and music in place by 7:45. No waitstaff should remain!

To: Clarissa
Please have the flowers we discussed in place by 7:30.

To: Room Service and Housekeeping
Please complete turndown service in the Pop Suite by 8:00 p.m. Make sure to pick up the music selections from my office before going to the suite. Please make sure the champagne is in the Pop Suite by 9:30 p.m. Well Chilled!!!

TRACE HEADED DOWN to the lower-level offices, thinking about his conversation with Nicholas. The old man was a master manipulator, and he never hesitated to use emotional blackmail to get what he wanted. Trace had never had qualms about doing the same, so why was he hesitant about using what he knew about Piper's vulnerabilities to get her to change the motif of the hotel? In the long run, she'd be better off. She'd have a legitimate success on her hands, and she'd have all that money to pursue whatever crazy schemes she wanted. And yet, there was something about this project that put a fire in her eyes. Even he had to admit that she'd done a good job. Hush was as nice as any Devon hotel. If it weren't for the sex business.

Of course there was more of the hotel for him to see, but he doubted there would be serious issues. Again, it was the emphasis on sex that skewed everything.

He'd take a quick glance at Exhibit A, the bar downstairs. Piper called it a sofa bar. There was a stage and a circular lounge. Sofas, private booths, liquor, candles. And on that stage? Naked people. Dancing. At least he hoped it was just dancing.

He tried to picture what it would be like, but his imagination wasn't up to the task. Or perhaps it was too vivid. It had to be illegal for people to have sex on stage, and Piper wasn't going to risk the hotel over something like that. But was it illegal for those watching the show to go for it right there?

He got out of the elevator and made his way to Piper's office. It was all he could do to bring his focus back to the matter at hand. The PR people were waiting, as

was Angela. She showed him to the conference room.
He wasted no time.

After brief introductions he put his briefcase on the
table and faced Kit Prescott, who was Piper's in-house
head of PR and the outside team of Tami Bressler and
Alison Fife, all of whom were young and the epitome
of New York chic. "Piper Devon hired you," he said,
"but I'm the one who holds the power. And if you want
to keep this account, I suggest you listen very carefully
to what I have to say."

PIPER LEFT the spa, pleased that Eartha Kitty was in
such good hands. Her pet concierge would be there in
an hour. Her name was Ruth Gaylor, and she was perfect. She loved animals, had taken care of them all her
life, and she was thrilled at the opportunity to make
Hush a welcome home to all the pets her guests would
bring. At the moment, she was shopping, buying all
kinds of wonderful beds and toys and treats to stock the
pet suite, and in the next couple of days everything
would be in place. She was even going to train her as-
sistants in the art of pet massage. No expense was being
spared, because Piper knew from experience that her clientele didn't just like their pets, they worshipped them.

It said a great deal that while Hush provided refer-
rals to babysitters, there had been no requests made by
any of the booked guests. But over a dozen were paying the extra fee for pet services.

Piper knew this town, knew the kind of people who
would stay at Hush. Rich, pampered, and always seek-

ing the next thrill. And what could be more thrilling than decadent sex? It was the one constant, the thing that never went out of style.

And wherever there were celebrities and sex, there would be fascination. Enough to keep the hotel alive in the press for years to come. Although she fully intended to keep the paparazzi away, stories would leak, people would talk. They always did. So why the hell not use it to her advantage? She'd been followed by the tabloid jackals since the day she was born. It was time for them to give something back.

She glanced at her watch. She'd left Trace alone with her PR people too long, and she hurried to the conference room. As she walked in, the conversation came to an abrupt halt. Kit, Tami and Alison looked right at her, and Piper knew instantly Trace had done something underhanded. The women looked guilty as sin, and Tami was even blushing. Trace didn't bother to look up. Even so, there was something smug in his passive expression.

"Would you ladies excuse us for a few moments?" Piper asked.

The team left with alarming speed.

"All right. What did you say to them?"

"Nothing I haven't said to you."

She sat down across from him. "You told them to ignore the sex angle."

"I did."

"It's my hotel, Trace. Not yours. Not my father's."

"The sex angle is going to kill your hotel."

She took deep breaths, unwilling to show him how

furious she was. But she had to put her hands on her lap so he wouldn't see her shake. "Okay, I was willing to try this. I even believed you when you said you'd give me a week. I think we both realize that was a blatant lie. The bottom line is, I'm not going to change into some-one else, Trace, and I'm not going to give in on the hotel. So why don't you go upstairs, pack your bags and go tell Daddy that the trial is officially over." She stood, headed for the door.

"Don't be ridiculous," Trace said as he grabbed her arm. "I'm trying to help you here."

"No, you're not. You're trying to manipulate me."

"Oh, and you're not?"

She wanted to deny it, but they both knew he was right. "I kept my part of the bargain."

He looked at his hand on her arm, and pulled away as if he'd been burnt. Then his gaze moved to hers, and his expression changed into something she didn't recog-nize. "Why did you decide to build a hotel?"

The question threw her. "What?"

"You could have done anything with the money you got on your twenty-fifth birthday. Anything that would have made money. Stocks, land development, fine art in-vestment. Anything."

"I know hotels. Remember? Daughter of Nicholas Devon?"

"Exactly. You chose to compete with him. Why is that?"

"So now you're psychoanalyzing me? Don't even."

"Come on, Piper. You built a hotel in the city where your father is the king of hotels. You agreed to the terms.

You knew full well that Nicholas would be appalled at the sex angle, so that's what you went for, full throttle."

"And your point is?"

"I don't believe you're seeing clearly. I think you're so busy subconsciously trying to rebel against your father that you don't know the mistake you're making."

"You're wrong."

"Am I?"

"What I offered you yesterday wasn't just a way to get you into bed or to manipulate you with sex. I meant it with all my heart. You can't see Hush the way I do because you're looking through the eyes of Nicholas Devon. Give my way a chance."

"Why should I, when you're not giving me the same courtesy?"

"Tell me what to do, and I'll do it."

"Do you mean that?"

She nodded. "I'll be as open as I can be. And if I'm wrong, I'll admit it. I just don't know what I can do to prove it."

"Sit down with me and go over my ideas for the hotel."

"To make it into a Devon?"

"A compromise."

She stood up, walked over to the credenza and poured herself a glass of water. She was in no rush to drink it as she thought about his proposition. Basically, she had to accept. But she seriously doubted she could be open enough to listen to what Trace had to say. He wanted to take away the very thing that made Hush her hotel. He wanted to make it something other, something bland, like every other Devon hotel, and the thought made her sick to her stomach.

But how could she ask him to be open to her if she couldn't reciprocate?

She turned. "All right. I can't promise to agree with you, but I'll do my very best to listen with an open mind."

"That's all I can ask for."

"Are you willing to do the same?"

He didn't answer her for a while. He stared at the painting on the wall behind her, his forehead creased, a slight frown curving his lips. "As long as we're putting it all out on the table…." He stood up, went over to her and sat back on the credenza, his gaze unflinching as he stared into her eyes. "Last night was remarkable. I was…" He shook his head. "I want a repeat performance very much. But I'm not sure that's the best way for us to approach this."

"Do you have any suggestions?"

"Not a one."

"So?"

"So why don't we ask the ladies to come back in. We'll go over what I told them, and then you take it from there. Our first foray into the world of compromise."

"And tonight?"

"Tonight, you can show me why lovers will be beating down your doors." He stuck out his hand.

She nodded. It was a start. Maybe she'd win and maybe she'd lose, but she truly believed Trace was going to try. And dammit, so would she. She put her hand in his.

The touch was meant to be all business. But they both knew that their particular business had a hell of a lot to do with pleasure. "This is weird."

"Very."

"But not...horrible."

He grinned. It made him look so much younger than his thirty-eight years. "You make me blush, Ms. Devon."

"It's my job."

"So I've gathered."

She realized her hand was still in his, and suddenly it was she who was blushing. She slipped away. "I'll go get them."

He cleared his throat, which made her smile. But when they all sat down, she felt oddly energized. Willing. Anxious for the day to end and for night to come.

AT SIX-FIFTEEN, they were finished with their meetings. Trace was in his suite, debating his next move. He and Piper had gone their separate ways an hour ago, and he wasn't sure if she was finished with the concierge meeting or not. But he wanted dinner and he wanted it with her.

He pulled out his cell and dialed hers. It rang four times and he got her voice mail. "Hey, it's Trace. Call me when you're done. I'm going to the gym. I thought we might go out for a bite."

He hung up, surprised that once he'd mentioned the gym the idea appealed so strongly. He'd been too stationary today, meeting after meeting. Lunch had been heavy, and he needed to move.

It didn't take him long to get ready, and then he was off, hoping he'd have the place to himself. He passed a couple of employees in the hallway, but the workout room was his.

He stretched for a while, thinking about what they'd accomplished today. He had to admit, Piper had been a lot more reasonable than he'd expected. She'd listened to him, and hadn't automatically cut his ideas to shreds. She hadn't rolled over, either. They'd discussed. Okay, argued. But it was reasonable. Thoughtful, even. Who'd have thought?

Not him. Between last night and today, a lot of things had changed. Mostly, his perception of a woman he'd known for so long that he'd thought he had her figured out. But he hadn't. Not really. She'd surprised him over and over.

He went to the treadmill and set it up to his specifications. It took his concentration for a few minutes, and then he went into automatic pilot. Of course, his thoughts returned to Piper.

How much did he really know about her? That she was a Devon, that she had a wild streak in her a mile wide. That she loved and hated her father. That she was much smarter than he'd imagined. And why would he think of her as smart? Whenever he heard about her it was for some stupid stunt. She'd embarrassed herself on several continents. Yeah, she'd done well in school, but frankly, he'd assumed that was all favoritism.

Her performance today had shown him there was actually a cunning brain at work. Which really just confirmed a secret hope. She'd built this hotel, for God's sake, and if she'd get with the program it would be a tremendous asset.

So why, if she was this bright, this savvy, had she hooked up with a loser like Logan Barrister? It wasn't that he was the exception, but the rule. She'd always been with flashy, stupid men. Musicians, actors, models. Good-looking men who couldn't scratch their own asses without cue cards.

She was better than that, better than what the tabloids made of her. But then, maybe she was holding back that wild side until the hotel was open. Angela had told him Logan's band would be coming to New York next month, so maybe the fireworks would fly then.

He just wished he understood her.

Oh well, it didn't matter as long as he did his job. If Piper could come out of it with a successful hotel and her inheritance, great. They'd all win. But no matter what, he had no intention of losing.

PIPER STOOD just to the side of the window that looked into the gym. Her gaze was fixed on Trace running on the treadmill. His T-shirt was wet, so was his hair. He looked damn fine.

She was going to have him tonight. In the pool and if she was lucky, again in her bed. Her whole body was thrilled.

Today had been fascinating. Trace had been true to

his word. He'd listened, and he'd only been a jerk a couple of times, which for Trace was saying something.

But tonight it was all her show. She wanted to show him what Hush could be like for lovers. She'd arranged a few surprises on the roof. Nothing that a good customer couldn't get, if so inclined. She wanted him to be swept away with the ambiance, the magic, the entire experience.

She wanted him to be swept away by her.

She'd better get started. She would go to her room, get showered and changed. He'd mentioned wanting dinner, but she'd taken care of that already.

Tonight was for lovers, and she felt like one as she headed for the elevator. It may only be for four more nights, but she would make each one count.

9

TRACE WAS DRAWN to the pool by the mellow sound of Frank Sinatra crooning "The Summer Wind" from invisible speakers.

The pool looked amazing with its underwater lights. The rest of the large space was lit dimly, mostly by candles and the wall sconces. Instead of chlorine, the air had been scented lightly with flowers, something sweet and exotic. He felt as though he was on an island, a safe haven away from the real world.

He wondered where Piper was. She'd left him a message on his cell, telling him to meet her here at 8:00. He was on time.

He'd showered after his workout, put on something easy and casual, which was evidently a good choice for this pool-side dinner.

Walking slowly, he went to the edge of the pool and looked down into the water. It was so inviting he regretted not bringing his trunks. On the other hand, there was no one here. Why not?

Just as he was about to take off his jacket, something made him turn.

Piper. Jeez. She looked incredible. His gaze moved down her body. The dress, long, sleeveless and with a low-scooped neckline, fit her like a second skin. It was red, and the material shimmered. He could see the hard jut of her nipples, the curve of her hips.

"Hungry?" she asked.

He laughed. "Oh, yeah."

"Good." She walked past him and he let himself savor the line of her back, the way the material contoured over her delicious behind.

She stopped across the pool at one of the white tables. As he approached he saw a champagne bucket, several domed platters, candles glittering in the dim light.

"A special treat from Amuse Bouche," she said as he held her chair.

He sat down across from her, liking the direction of the evening more and more. He poured them each champagne as she uncovered dishes. Lobster morsels, saffron rice, wild mushrooms. "It looks wonderful."

She served him on the plates he recognized from the restaurant, then fixed a dish for herself. Sinatra kept singing.

They ate for a few minutes. He couldn't remember when he'd felt so relaxed, which was interesting because the awareness of Piper seeped into every part of him, his hands, his chest, and of course, his cock, half-hard with anticipation.

"What's that smile for?"

"This is great," he said. "Is this service available to all the guests or just you?"

"No, anyone can reserve the pool after hours."

"Wow."

"But there's something you should know."

"What's that?"

Her lips glistened. "There's no shoptalk allowed poolside."

"I see."

"None at all."

"So what does that leave us with?"

She stabbed a piece of lobster and chewed it delicately. "I guess that leaves us. Which might be interesting, if we let it."

"Interesting, how?"

"Well, how much do we really know about each other?" she asked. "I've known you for years, but only in one context. There's a great deal about you that's a mystery."

"Me? Not really."

"Yes, you. For example, this music. Do you like it?"

"Love it. I'm a big fan of the Chairman of the Board."

"What else?"

God, her eyes where intoxicating. Blue and questioning, fantastic in candlelight. "I don't like country," he said. "Or hip-hop. Or show tunes."

"Hmm. Okay, what do you like?"

"Classic rock, Mayer, Linkin Park, Usher."

Her brows went up in surprise.

"What?"

"I don't know. I guess I never think of you listening to anything modern."

"Excuse me? I'm not that much older than you."

"I know. But you act like—" She stopped. Concentrated on her food.

"I act like…?"

"Older, okay?"

"So you're saying I'm boring."

"No. Not exactly."

He leaned back. "This gets better and better."

"Well, I'm sorry, but whenever I see you, you're all business. I'll admit, your wit redeems you, but come on, Trace. Most of the time you act like one of Dad's old cronies."

He flushed as the arguments came to him rapid-fire. But he said none of them. After a hit of the cold champagne, his temper cooled enough to admit that she had a point. "It's my job."

She leaned over and put her hand on his. "I know. Hence the questions. Tell me about the part that's not your job."

He looked at her fingers, so long and beautiful, and thought about how much he wanted the dinner to end and dessert to start. But this was probably a good thing. Talking, getting to know each other. Perhaps if she didn't perceive him as the enemy, she'd be more willing to listen to him.

"Well?"

"There's not much to say. Work is pretty consuming."

"You have days off. Vacations."

"Not many."

"Trace."

"Okay," he said, missing her hand the moment she went back to her meal. "I play tennis. Golf. I like going to Central Park."

"Where?"

"I don't know. I walk around Strawberry Fields sometimes. Go to the model boat pond."

"The zoo?"

"It's usually too crowded for me. But I like to skate."

Her fork clattered to her plate. "You in-line skate?"

"Yeah. Why are you so shocked?"

She laughed. "I had this image of you in your three-piece Armani, wearing a helmet and knee pads."

"I own jeans."

"You do not."

"Hey."

"I've never seen them. Not that you don't look smashing in your casual chic, but it's not jeans and a T-shirt."

"Jesus, you really do think I'm an old fart."

She smiled as she looked at him, and despite her message, he wouldn't have wanted to be anywhere else on the planet. But then her delight shifted into something else. Sadness? He wasn't sure.

"People make assumptions," she said, her voice tinged with melancholy. "They only see what's easy. Or what's available, I suppose. But once they've made up their minds…"

"I think this might be the first time we've ever talked about something other than business."

She nodded, then sat for a long moment staring at a candle. Then she smiled again. "Did you bring any jeans?"

He shook his head. "I'm here on business."

"Do you really have jeans?"

"Of course."

"Do you get them pressed at the dry cleaners?"

"What difference does that make?"

"It doesn't, I suppose. Only…"

"What?"

"I think you'd look really hot in faded jeans with a few well-placed tears."

"I'll rip some the moment I get home."

She was back. Teasing Piper was better than anything. Even better than pissed-off Piper, who was also more fun than she should be.

"Now are you going to tell me you have ripped, faded jeans?" he asked.

"I do, actually."

"Purchased that way?"

"Nope. Worn out."

"I've never seen them."

"No, you haven't. Grunge is part of my private life."

He laughed. "What private life? You're the most photographed person in the world."

"No, I'm not. I'm actually number four, but that's beside the point. I do have secrets, Trace. What the world sees doesn't represent everything that I am."

"Why don't you want people to know you're smart?"

The smile she gave him made the candles seem dim. "Good one, Winslow. Very good."

"Cut it out and tell me."

She sipped some champagne. He was surprised at

how much she'd eaten. She rarely ate much. A bite or two of everything, then lots of water. Most of the women he knew did the same. He wondered if she ever just pigged out. Ate a box of donuts or a gallon of ice cream.

"It works for me," she said. "With the public, at least. I just give them what they want, and no one presses for more. I have no interest in sharing myself with the world. That wasn't a choice."

"But your image is."

She shook her head. "That's not remotely true."

"Come on, Piper. I've seen the photos. No one forced you to go out and get wasted."

Her lips pressed together and her gaze shifted. "New rule. We're not allowed to talk about the press, either."

He nodded. "Sorry. You're right. I want the same thing you do. I want to know who you are."

"Ask me."

"Do you read?"

She nodded.

"What's your favorite book?"

"*East of Eden,*" she said.

He was surprised. Not only at her answer, but at how ready she was with it. "No kidding."

"You?"

"*Shogun.*"

"Ah. Manipulation. Intrigue. I'm not surprised."

"At least it wasn't *The Art of War.*"

"No, it wasn't."

"Movie?" he asked.

"Tie between *To Kill a Mockingbird* and *Raiders of the Lost Ark.*"

He laughed, hard.

"What's so funny?"

"Not close to what I expected," he said. "Not close."

"Good."

He looked at her shining eyes. "Yeah, it is good."

"You ready for the next part of our adventure?"

He grinned. "I am."

"Okay then." She stood up, walked over to the huge spa and pressed a few buttons. The engines running the jets were surprisingly quiet. The music, which had changed to some contemporary jazz, still swirled around the pool.

Piper stepped away from the spa, smiled at him. Then she pulled her dress slowly up her body.

He forgot to breathe as he saw that she was naked. Totally, completely naked. Except for her heels. It was a damn fine look. Dessert had never been more tempting.

SHE WATCHED HIM take off his clothes. First, the sports jacket, then the dark blue shirt which made his eyes look so sexy. His chest. Oh, God. It was a work of art. Just looking at it made her want to touch him, to run her hands slowly up and down with her eyes closed so that nothing got in the way of all the texture and form.

She sighed as he undid his belt. That was in her personal top ten erotic moments. The Undoing of the Belt. It was such a simple act, a prelude to so much. Fingers specific, the softest hiss of leather, which, while she couldn't hear at the moment, her memory provided like a tiny gift. Then the button, one handed, and the slow drag of the zipper.

He toed off his shoes, and let his pants pool at his feet. Mmm, she liked the black silk boxers. She laughed.

He quirked his head. "Um, not the best time to be laughing at a guy."

She waved her hand as she walked closer. "I was just thinking that Boy Scouts could camp under that tent."

He looked down. Threw his hands up in shock. "Oh, my God. What's happening? It just keeps growing."

It might not be the best time to laugh, but she loved this. Laughter, good conversation, music, the soft, warm air. The world was hers, at least for the moment. All the burdens of her day had been left in the elevator. Tonight was for fun. For passion. For discovery. The only way Trace would see Hush as she did was if all their bullshit could be put on hold, at least for a little while.

He'd taken off his socks, and now his hands were at the waistband of his shorts. She stopped him with a kiss. She moved his hands, replacing them with her own. She lowered herself along with his underwear, revealing his hard, thick erection. "For me?" she whispered as she settled her knees on his crumpled pants.

"Piper…" His hand went to her cheek. He lifted her chin until he was looking deep into her eyes. "My God."

She smiled, then turned her attention to the proud beauty before her. The scent of sex mixed with flowers. Her thumb dipped in the pearl of moisture, spreading it over the mushroom head. She tried to think of anything she'd ever touched that was quite as silky, but she couldn't come up with a thing. Wrapping her fingers around him, she stroked him all the way down, then back up again.

He moaned above her and when she steadied herself with a hand on his hip, she felt him tremble. Such power. She could break him with a touch, with her lips and her tongue.

But that wasn't what she wanted. Not to break him, but to learn him. To feel his blood pulse, hear his harsh breath, the sound of his need.

She leaned forward and ran her tongue in a circle around the head. Her eyes closed as she let her other senses take over. He smelled so wonderful. Clean and spicy. And then there was that undercurrent, that ozone smell of lust.

Her lips closed over him and she rubbed her tongue on the sensitive underside, waited for his gasp, for the shiver to run through his body. Wondered if he could feel her smile.

Taking him as deeply as she could, she pleasured him, loving this, feeling naked and erotic and aching.

His hands went to her face, but his touch was light, a gentle caress, following as her head moved back and forth. She wondered if he watched her, or if his eyes were closed, his head thrown back.

Her own were still shut, but she could tell that if she didn't stop soon, he was going to come. It wasn't time.

Giving one last long suck, she sat back. His hands dropped as he whimpered his disappointment.

"Don't worry, Trace," she said, rising to her feet. "This is just the beginning."

"I don't think I'll survive the ending."

"Sure you will." She turned. "Follow me."

He did. She glanced back and grinned at his distress. Not a terribly nice thing to do, she knew, but it was too heady to resist.

She reached the side of the spa which was churning with bubbles and heat. In a few steps, she was waist-deep and sighing with pure bliss. She sank down, the bubbles jetting into all the right places.

"You stopped that for this?"

She turned her head to see Trace standing at the side of the spa, looking daggers at her. "Yep."

"Fine," he said. "Swell." He climbed in, wincing as he settled close. "You're a cruel woman, Piper Devon."

"Yes, I am."

"You don't have to be so smug about it."

"Why not? It's fun. I so rarely get to see the immediate response to one of my devious plots."

"Exactly what is your devious plot?"

She leaned over and kissed him. Not a minor kiss, either, but deep and full and long. And that wasn't all. She touched him again, grasped his erection, pumped him as she thrust her tongue. When she was about ready to come herself, she pulled away. "I'm going to make you forget your own name," she said, her lips real close to his ear. Then she stuck her tongue there, too.

He turned around to kiss her again, but she wanted to keep up the tension so she reached for yet another bottle of chilled champagne. There were glasses, but the hell with them. She popped the cork and drank from the bottle.

His mouth was open, his eyes wild. "You…you…"

"I think the word you're looking for is *bitch.*"

"I would never say that."

"But you'd think it."

"True."

She grinned. Handed him the Cristal. "Relax, big guy. We've got hours."

He took a long drink, then put the bottle back in its ice. When he looked at her again, his eyes held mischief. "You know, two can play at this game."

"Oh?"

He nodded. And she felt his hand on her thigh. "Be afraid," he said, his voice a low growl. "Be very afraid."

10

TRACE CLOSED his eyes, concentrating on the hot water bubbling against his body instead of Piper's hand. Which was not easy.

He'd been on the edge for what seemed like hours, and he had to do something about it soon. He tried to recall the last time he'd been so frustrated and was somewhat surprised to realize it had been years. Since college. When he was alone, he took care of things himself, and when he had company, he was in control so when he wanted to wrap it up, he wrapped it up.

Usually, he was the one using delaying tactics, taking his companion to the brink over and over. He had to admit, this turnaround had its good points, although it was time now to go back to the natural order of things. As soon as he could calm down a bit more, he'd show Piper a thing or two.

He was still amazed at how surprising the day had been, and tonight had surpassed all his expectations. He'd never envisioned a relaxed evening, one where he didn't feel he had to watch every word, that was all parry and thrust. He smiled, thinking about the other kind of parry and thrust. That would definitely play a major role in the remainder of the night.

"What are you grinning about?"

He opened his eyes to find her staring at him. There was a softness to her face that reminded him of when she'd been a young girl. "You. Us." He nodded toward the dinner table. "It's nice."

"I know," she said. "I'm pretty stunned by it all, too." She reached back to snag the champagne. "Do you think it's just the sex?"

"That's got to be a big part of it," he said, not as taken aback as he should be at his own candor. "We've been dodging this bullet for years."

"I know." She took a drink. "While we're being so cozy I wanted to tell you—" she turned to him once more "—I'm sorry."

"For what?"

"I was a kid. I shouldn't have put you in such an awkward position. Your job, everything. It was wrong, and I apologize."

He nodded, remembering again the night she'd offered herself to him. Of course, he hadn't touched her. It would have been wrong on so many levels, but damn, he'd had a moment there… "It's okay. I was flattered."

"Flattered?"

He grinned. "It wasn't easy to walk away. It was maybe the nicest invitation I'd ever had."

"Really?"

"Really."

"So why did you? Walk away, I mean."

"You were a kid."

"It wasn't just the job?"

"That was a factor. I won't lie to you. I'd just started, and I was pretty green. But no. It wasn't. You'd had a lot of champagne. I couldn't."

"I was devastated."

"I'm sorry."

"I got over it."

He frowned. He didn't like to think about how she'd gone about getting over it. Her sex life had been plastered in papers all over the world. "I'm just sorry I couldn't have been more of a friend."

"Whatever we have, Trace, I don't think you could ever call it friendship."

"So what's this?"

She shook her head. "I don't know. And for tonight, I don't care."

He took her by the shoulders and pulled her into his arms. The water made it easy to position her just so. Neatly between his legs so he could feel her chest, so she cradled his cock against her stomach. "You're right," he said. "No thinking." Then he kissed her.

She opened her mouth to his questing tongue, then responded almost shyly. This wasn't the woman who'd taken him on her knees. There was a sweetness and a vulnerability that he'd thought had vanished years ago.

Suddenly the water was too hot, the music too loud. "Come on," he said. "Let's get out of here."

She stood. The water cascaded down her body, dripped from her firm nipples and he couldn't help but lean forward and take the hard nub in his mouth. As his tongue circled the areola, he could feel her get harder, all the little bumps and ridges that surrounded the nipple itself reacted to his caress, and he knew she was getting harder elsewhere. He wanted to taste that, too, but he couldn't when she was under water.

He let her go, and as he leaned back her fingers stroked the side of his face.

Then she climbed out of the pool, and he followed. There were two large towels, and even though it was chilly now, dripping as they were, she wrapped a towel around him first.

With unexpected tenderness, she dried him, patting and rubbing his back, his chest, then lower.

He felt her shiver and stopped her, folding the towel around her body, hating to hide it but wanting her comfortable and dry.

The music was almost as soft as her skin as he helped her into her dress.

He put on his clothes and as he did, he studied Piper. He faced her profile. Long, lean, perfectly proportioned. She had a small scar on her shoulder, and he wondered how she'd injured herself. His gaze moved to her face. Someone had once done an article about that face, about the symmetry. Everything in its place, as if it had been shaped by a master sculptor.

He'd heard other women talk about her. How it was so unfair for one person to be so blessed. Money, looks, power. They blamed Piper for her good fortune, and they resented her for it, too.

He'd only seen Piper with one girlfriend in all the years he'd known her. Lisa Scott. Who was also beautiful and accomplished.

Did Piper want more friends? It had never once occurred to Trace that she could be lonely, but she must be. She didn't lack for groupies and wannabes, but that wasn't the same.

But it wasn't his problem, was it? He didn't need to be her friend. He needed to get the job done. If having mind-blowing sex was part of it, oh, well. He'd have to deal. But it didn't mean things were going to change. Piper was the daughter of his boss. Once the hotel issue was settled, it would be over between them.

He finished dressing. Enough. He wanted her and the wait was killing him. He hadn't forgotten her teasing from before. She thought she knew where the night was heading.

She had no idea.

Once they were decent, both of them carrying their shoes, they headed to the elevator. She pressed the button for her floor.

They didn't speak. But they did touch. Her head against the crook of his neck, his arm around her slim shoulders. He felt her breathe, thought about everything he wanted to do with her. To her.

Inside her suite, he stopped her, turned her back to the door, kissed her as he grabbed her wrists and forced them up above her head.

She gasped as he pinned her with his body, so tightly

GET FREE BOOKS and a FREE GIFT WHEN YOU PLAY THE...

SLOT MACHINE GAME!

Just scratch off the silver box with a coin. Then check below to see the gifts you get!

YES! I have scratched off the silver box. Please send me the 2 free Harlequin Blaze™ books and gift for which I qualify. I understand I am under no obligation to purchase any books, as explained on the back of this card.

350 HDL D7W4   **150 HDL D7XJ**

FIRST NAME	LAST NAME

ADDRESS

APT.#	CITY

STATE/PROV.	ZIP/POSTAL CODE

7	7	7	**Worth TWO FREE BOOKS plus a BONUS Mystery Gift!**
🍒	🍒	🍒	**Worth TWO FREE BOOKS!**
♣	♣	♣	**Worth ONE FREE BOOK!**
🔔	🔔	🍒	**TRY AGAIN!**

www.eHarlequin.com

(H-B-04/05)

DETACH AND MAIL CARD TODAY!

The Harlequin Reader Service® — Here's how it works:

Accepting your 2 free books and gift places you under no obligation to buy anything. You may keep the books and gift and return the shipping statement marked "cancel." If you do not cancel, about a month later we'll send you 4 additional books and bill you just $3.99 each in the U.S., or $4.47 each in Canada, plus 25¢ shipping & handling per book and applicable taxes if any.* That's the complete price and — compared to cover prices of $4.75 each in the U.S. and $5.75 each in Canada — it's quite a bargain! You may cancel at any time, but if you choose to continue, every month we'll send you 4 more books, which you may either purchase at the discount price or return to us and cancel your subscription.

*Terms and prices subject to change without notice. Sales tax applicable in N.Y. Canadian residents will be charged applicable provincial taxes and GST. Credit or debit balances in a customer's account(s) may be offset by any other outstanding balance owed by or to the customer.

he could feel the press of her breasts against his chest, the hollow between her thighs.

Finished with games, he ravished her mouth.

Piper took his punishing kiss and gave it right back. She pushed her hips against him, rubbed his erection, wishing they were both naked again, wishing he would take her, right here up against the wall.

Piper loved being helpless, loved the abandon, but she couldn't let go. Not with Trace, despite their conversation. There was too much history to let herself fall completely.

So she bit his lower lip just hard enough to make him jerk, to make him understand he couldn't call all the shots.

He backed up, still keeping her hands above her head, pressed against the wall. He stared at her with darkened eyes, his lips curled in a wicked smile.

He said nothing. Instead, his hands abruptly dropped. The next thing she knew she was in his arms, and she had to grab his neck as he took her through the suite to the bedroom.

He put her down next to the bed, stepped back and waited.

"Why, Mr. Winslow," she said as she stripped for him once more. "You are full of surprises."

Trace laughed as he shed his clothes. "Who was it that said people see what they want to see?" he said, his voice, sandpaper and silk, thrilling her as much as the challenge in his gaze. "Lay down. Don't cover yourself. I want to see every inch of you."

She wasn't quite sure how she felt about this new Trace, but her body had definite opinions in the affirmative. She spread herself across the silk bedspread, lifted her arms until her hands curled around the wood of the headboard, and even as her face heated in a wild blush, she spread her legs and lifted her hips.

His moan turned into a wry chuckle as he climbed onto the bed, right between her spread legs. "You, my dear Piper, are evil. And, I might add, you have wiles."

"Wiles?"

"A deceitful or seductive manner."

"How can you possibly claim this is deceitful? I'm offended."

"Because you're turning into someone completely new right before my eyes."

"Is this a good thing?"

He moved up her body, their skin barely touching. His heat infused her, his gaze held her transfixed. "Oh, yeah."

She gasped in each breath, her breasts rising and falling rapidly as he moved in for the kill. But she still had one trick up her sleeve.

She wrapped her legs around his waist, locking them together at the ankles. Squeezing, she held him fast, delighting in his astonishment.

Then, using his body for leverage, she lifted her hips. His swollen erection was caught just above her mound, and she rubbed him, hard.

"Shit," he whispered.

She laughed at his breathlessness, using all her muscles to maintain control. She had him, helpless, even though she never released her hold above her head.

He took her mouth again, a searing kiss that made her

lose her rhythm. His tongue thrust, filling her. And then he pushed back, breaking her hold. Her legs went down to the bed, and he was up on his knees.

He inched up until she couldn't see past him. He towered above her, but this wasn't anything like her little tease out by the pool. He held her chest down with his thighs, with the weight of his stare.

His hand went to his cock and he stroked himself slowly, from the base to the crown, a quick finger over the slick, and back down again.

He was hard and hot, and all she could think of was what it would feel like inside her. God, she wanted him. She hadn't felt this…excitement in so long. It wasn't just physical, either. She wasn't the only one with wiles.

Keeping her still between his knees, he reached for the night table and came back with a condom. She hated them, wished they didn't need to use them, but even that couldn't dim her anticipation.

He rolled the condom on. She could see his need, his desire, on his stunning face, in his brilliant eyes.

He leaned over, his lips coming close, but not touching hers. "Don't move," he whispered.

Oh, she wouldn't. Every part of her wanted this, couldn't wait. He stirred between her thighs once more, and his hands cupped her legs, then lifted them to his shoulders. He smiled at her with so much arrogance she nearly screamed, and then he thrust inside her, all the way, so deep the whole bed moved, and she did scream.

He stayed there for a minute, dragging in a deep breath, then he withdrew, slowly.

"Come on, Trace," she said, knowing she was edging toward danger, but loving it. Loving that her mind was as turned on as her body. "You can do better than that."

He laughed. "Better?"

"Show me what you've got."

He slammed back into her, making her cry out again. Making her back arch and her body tremble.

"Is that what you want?"

She opened her eyes again. "More."

"Oh, you're asking for it, missy."

"I'm so scared." She pulled her head up off the pillow. "Can't you feel me shaking?"

He shook his head. "That's not shaking," he whispered. His tempo changed as he thrust faster, leaning over her so she was almost bent double, his penetration stealing every thought she'd ever had.

"This is shaking," he said.

She cried out, gripping the headboard so hard she thought she might rip the bed apart.

"Come on, Piper." His lips were just above hers.

She let go of the headboard and clawed his back as her body began the fabulous convulsions of the most intense orgasm she'd ever had.

He woke with a gasp, his heart pounding in his chest, his body hot as hell and trembling. He threw back the covers and stood. When his feet touched the floor, he realized where he was and that he wasn't dying of a heart attack but waking from a nightmare.

He hadn't disturbed Piper, which was a good thing.

It was so damn late. Actually, early. Almost four. He needed something to drink.

It took him a minute to get into the living room, and he closed the bedroom door behind him. God, he was sweating. His heart still hadn't slowed, and now, shit, the images from his dream were coming back.

He turned on the light, wincing as his eyes adjusted. The fridge was stocked with everything from champagne to tomato juice, but he grabbed a bottle of water and drank most of it standing in the cool air from the open refrigerator.

He gasped as he brought the bottle down. He hadn't had the dream in years. Why now? What the hell was going on?

After he closed the door, he went over to one of the large leather chairs. He was still naked, and he didn't have a robe with him, but at this point he didn't care.

Hissing as his overheated skin met the cool of the leather, he stared out the huge window at the dark night. Of course there were lights on, it was Manhattan.

He'd grown up here and probably couldn't function anywhere else, but still. There were times when he wondered what else his life could have been.

His father had worked for Devon all his adult life. The firm, Winslow, Reynolds and Webster, had no other clients. It was a way of life, one Trace had been indoctrinated to from childhood. The Devon hotel chain kept his family in sports cars and luxury apartments, and he had few complaints. Sure, he'd wanted something more ambitious, but that was when he was a kid. He'd actually wanted to specialize in family law, and back then he'd been naive enough to think that he could make a difference.

Of course, life had taught him otherwise, but some stubborn, stupid part of him still had remnants of that old folly. And every once in a great while, he entertained thoughts. Though admittedly, not for long.

Something had stirred those dinosaurs tonight, and that's why he'd dreamed about Bob Steiner. His old college roommate, and his closest friend.

At least he used to be. Before he'd killed himself.

Bob had gotten himself in trouble. Insider trading, fraud and embezzlement. He'd never told Trace why. What had happened to him. In college he'd been an idealist, and honest as the day was long. But something had obviously happened in the five years after graduation.

They'd lost touch. Not completely, but they were both so busy trying to build their careers that everything, including friendship, had been very low on the priority list.

The last he'd heard from Bob had been right around the time of his promotion. Nicholas had made him acting administrator of all the Devon trusts, and his days and nights had been consumed with learning all he could.

Bob had called one night, and goddamn it, he'd been crying. Crying. It had been so out of character that Trace should have understood right then. But he hadn't. Bob had told him he was in trouble. He hadn't gone into the details. Just had asked Trace for legal help.

And what had Trace done for his old friend?

Shrugged him off. Trace had told him he was too busy, had to go out of town, and gave him the name of another lawyer.

Bob had hung up the phone, probably feeling even more distraught and ashamed by the lack of a caring response from him.

The next time Trace thought about the phone call, he'd been contacted by a reporter from the *New York Times,* who'd notified him of Bob's suicide and asked for comments. Hearing that, Trace had felt sick with guilt.

It had taken a long time, but Trace had finally understood he wasn't to blame. That he had no way of knowing just how bad off Bob had been.

But waves of guilt kept surging up from time to time. Like tonight. When he'd had the best sex of his life. When he'd discovered an entirely new side to someone he'd thought he understood. When life was about as good as it could get.

So why? Because things were good? Or because he was letting Piper influence him?

His instincts told him it was the latter. That he was starting to let his feelings get in the way of his job. Which was crazy.

He might like sex with Piper, but not enough to give up everything. No woman was worth that.

And as for his nightmare? He'd put it where it belonged. Behind him.

_11_

TRACE WALKED into Erotique to find that Piper was still being interviewed. He should go back to his room, get some work done, but he really didn't feel like it. He was tired after a long day of negotiations with the culinary workers. During the breaks he'd caught up on some contracts for a new Devon hotel in Belize.

He went to the bar and pulled up a stool next to Lisa Scott. "Who's that?"

"Jace Friedken," she said, leaning toward him but not shifting her gaze from Piper. _"Vanity Fair."_

Trace watched for a while, trying to reconcile the woman he watched now to the Piper he'd seen this afternoon.

She'd been tough-minded with the union officials, not letting them slide on one issue. But unlike her father, she hadn't tried to screw them, either. They'd walked out with a fair deal.

Her negotiating skills were top-notch, which was a surprise in itself. The union leader had swaggered in, expecting to eat Piper for lunch, and was soon eating crow instead when he saw Piper was on to his every trick.

What Trace wrestled with was what she'd given away. The benefits, in particular, were quite generous, above the standard in Manhattan. She'd told him she wanted employees who'd be loyal, but was it worth the money?

The only way to know would be to wait, but if Nicholas took over, the contract would change along with the hotel theme.

"Can I get you something?"

He turned at the sound of the bartender. She was an attractive woman with streaks of blue in her extravagant hair, but he liked her smile.

"Stoli, rocks, please." He touched Lisa's arm. "What about you?"

She ordered an apple martini. When the bartender had gone, Lisa looked at him questioningly. "Are you starting to get it?"

"Get what?"

"Hush. What Piper's trying to do."

He shook his head. "No, I'm not."

Lisa sighed. "It's going to work, you know. The whole concept is brilliant, and no one on earth could pull it off like Piper."

"You're her friend, of course you're going to see it that way."

"So because I like Piper, I'm stupid?"

"No, I didn't mean that at all."

"I did a hell of a lot of research on this hotel, Trace. But not half as much as Piper did. You have no idea what's gone into this."

"The woman knows hotels, I'll admit that, but she's still not seeing the big picture."

"And what is that?"

The drinks came and Trace paid. Then he turned back, watching as Piper laughed, smiled, charmed the reporter. "Nicholas has built an empire and a trademark. They're inextricably intertwined. Devon is a brand name and it's worth everything."

"It's not the Devon Hush."

"Doesn't matter. You can't separate Piper from Devon. It's a package and she's striking at the very heart of what's made Nicholas one of the richest men in the world. How can he possibly endorse this? It's like Trump opening a sex shop. It tarnishes more than the name."

Lisa turned to him. "You're here. You see that she's gone to tremendous lengths to make Hush a class act all the way."

"But the focus is still on sex. That overshadows anything else."

Lisa shook her head. "She's making her own mark, and she's doing it brilliantly."

"If she wasn't Piper Devon, it might work, but she is, and therefore it can't work."

"Taking this away is going to kill her."

"There's more at stake than Piper's pride."

"I think you're wrong. On all sorts of levels. She earned this, Trace. You have no idea."

"Look, I don't like it any more than you do, but it's the way it is."

The drinks were on the bar and Lisa got hers. "It's

the way it was. You and Nicholas are living in the past. I can understand her father, but frankly, you confuse the hell out of me."

He got his own drink, then turned his attention to Piper.

It was like watching a silent movie, something glamorous and entrancing. Piper's body language was perfect. The way she mirrored the reporter, her occasional touches creating a connection, her gaze on his. He knew how the guy was feeling. Snookered, completely, wanting nothing more than to be in her presence, special because he was the focus of all that energy.

Piper had a gift, and he wanted so much for her to put it to good use. Although he couldn't hear the conversation, he knew without a doubt that it centered on sex. Not simply Hush, but Piper's sexuality. As quality hotels were her father's trademark, sexuality was Piper's, and after her display of business acumen this afternoon, Trace was acutely aware that it didn't do her justice.

If only he could help her see that. To take herself seriously. But listening to her flirting laughter, he knew it wasn't the job of a few days, or even weeks.

She was so firmly rooted in her own image, she couldn't shift her perspective. And if she didn't, she was going to lose so much.

He wondered if this would be the final split between Piper and Nicholas. They'd never forgive each other, which was a damn shame. The only winner would be Kyle, and although he liked the kid, he wasn't the brightest bulb in the chandelier. Devon Industries would suffer. Nicholas knew that, which is why he'd brought out the big guns.

Lisa sighed.

"What's wrong?"

"She does it so effortlessly. They just melt. She turns them into mush at the first laugh."

"It's what she's been trained to do."

"She may have perfected the technique, but she was like this even as a kid. I know, I watched."

"You two have been friends for a long time."

"Forever."

He wondered at the sadness he heard behind the word. "It must have been difficult."

"Not really. I don't mind the shade."

Trace studied the woman who he'd never paid much attention to. She wasn't directly involved with Devon, so he'd only met her at the occasional party. She was attractive. Beautiful, really. Why hadn't he noticed that before? Dark hair, nice eyes and a lush mouth. She was a little on the skinny side, but then that's what all the women wanted, wasn't it? She'd grown up in Piper's shadow, and even after all these years, she was working for her friend. "Why'd you sign up?" he asked.

"I know hotels. I grew up in them, too."

"I know. But why here? Why with Piper?"

"She's my closest friend."

"You didn't want to find out what it would be like outside?"

"Not really. It's what I'm used to."

"Okay."

"What about you?"

He looked at her.

"You went into the family business. Didn't Piper tell me that you'd wanted to do something else? Family law?"

"That was years ago."

"No regrets?"

His gaze moved to Piper, who was listening to the reporter with her head slightly tilted to the side. She had on a white silky dress, something that hugged her curves and made her look otherworldly. He wanted her. So much it hurt. But, like her friend, his lot in life was to be the man in the background, the one who stepped in after, who cleaned up the messes. He might have Piper's attention this week, but only because she needed him. The moment the drama was over, he'd be back to a bit player. "Sometimes," he said.

"I see," Lisa said.

"What?"

She patted his hand. "It'll pass. The effect seems to be localized."

"What the hell are you talking about?"

"She has this effect on all men. Well, all straight men. No, I've actually seen it work on gay men, too. But when you're away for a while, it won't be so bad."

"Lisa, you're nuts."

"I may be. But I've also been around long enough to recognize The Piper Effect, and honey, you've got it bad."

Though he didn't want to admit it, she was right. He also noticed Lisa was staring hard at the reporter, and she had been for a while. "You know that guy?"

"Nope. Just met him today."

Trace took another drink, welcoming the spread of warmth as it slid down his throat. It occurred to him that it would be hard for Lisa to get any male attention while she was around Piper. And since she was around Piper all the time…

"Well, I have some work to do," she said, standing up. She straightened her jacket, grabbed her purse from the bar. "Tell Piper I'll see her in the morning."

"Sure you don't want to stay till the end of the interview? Maybe talk to Jace there. I'll bet he'd love to hear your thoughts on the hotel."

"Yeah, right. I'll see you, Trace."

He nodded. Watched her walk across the room. There was something going on there, but he wasn't sure what. Of course she was a woman and they were notoriously mysterious, especially the one who so perplexed him, sitting across the room, her legs crossed and her skirt up high enough to make a man salivate.

He'd managed to keep his mind on business most of the day. At odd times, though, once in the middle of a sentence, memories of her in bed would invade. Memories of Piper naked, the sounds she made, the way her neck arched, the taste of her inner thigh.

He'd blushed, even while he felt like a teenager for doing so. But he'd never been in this situation before, where sex and business were all wrapped up in one frustrating package. He'd worked for his father's law firm since college, and it had never come up. He'd never even been tempted to dip into the staff pool. Jesus, what was he doing? First law of business was don't think with your dick. Okay, second law. First law was know your opponent. Only in this case he wasn't quite sure who the opponent was.

Did he really want Piper to fail? No, absolutely not. But was changing her plan failing? Only in her eyes.

He looked at her, and for the first time since he'd come into the bar, she looked back. He wasn't sure if Jace was talking or not, but Piper's gaze connected with his for a startling second, and he caught this tiny little smile, barely more than a hint, and damn if he didn't feel his chest expand. It was as if he'd put something over on the *Vanity Fair* guy, that she'd slipped him a secret meant only for him.

He was turning into a woman, for God's sake. Finishing off his vodka, he stood up, not willing to sit by like some groupie for one more minute. If Piper wanted to get together with him later, she had his cell. He needed to go to his own place and pick up some things.

He also needed to get his mind out of bed and back on business. Nothing was settled, not a damn thing.

LISA WENT BACK to her office. She had a lot to do tonight, and she wanted to go down to the final dress rehearsal at Exhibit A.

Eddie Benjamin had been working his tail off, choreographing the dancing and putting together the music and light show for the basement bar.

It was a unique concept, at least for Manhattan. A lounge with a great deal of privacy for the clientele, de-

signed for couples, adults only. The music was sophisticated, the atmosphere rich with scent and exotic lights,
including lasers and black lights and a bunch of other
high-tech gizmos. But the main eye candy would be on
the stage. The most gorgeous men and women she'd
ever seen, professional dancers, dressed in almost nothing, and dances as close to sex as one could get and still
be dressed.

Which begged the question, why on earth was she so
anxious to see it? She had no one in her life, and there
wasn't going to be anyone in her life ever, so why bother?
It would only end up getting her all hot and bothered and
then what? Another evening with B.O.B.? The rate she
was going, she'd need to buy batteries by the case.

Dammit, she'd liked Jace.

She leaned back in her chair and stared at the stack
of applications waiting for her approval. It's not as if she
didn't like her job. She loved hiring and employee motivation and everything that went along with keeping a
hotel running smoothly. The job wasn't the issue. It was
her. At least in college, she'd had a chance with guys.
Until they found out who her best friend was. Until they
met Piper. Then she might as well have been a potted
plant for all they cared.

Who could blame them? Piper was everything, and
she'd yet to meet a woman who could compete. And
honestly, Lisa didn't mind. Except sometimes.

She'd sat in that bar and watched two men turn into
slavish pups just watching Piper. She wondered if Trace
knew just how bad he had it for his client. Despite his

earnest declarations about Nicholas Devon and how right he was, Trace was going to come around. There was no doubt in Lisa's mind at all.

But he'd go kicking and screaming, which was good, because Piper needed someone who wouldn't just fold.

At least she was through with Logan. Lisa shuddered. What an ass he was. But Piper didn't care. He was easy, and he deflected some of the glare.

But she'd be much better off with Trace. If she didn't blow it. Which she probably would, because despite Piper being one of the most wonderful humans ever, she was terminally stupid when it came to men.

Lisa opened the first file. As if she could talk. Oh, well. Being alone wasn't fatal. She'd get through it, just like always.

PIPER MADE IT to the suite before her smile collapsed. God, the interview had dragged on forever, but she thought it had gone pretty well. Who cared? It was publicity, and she had no control over the press. None whatsoever. She had no control over a hell of a lot of things.

She wished she hadn't been so distracted, though. It had been fine during the meetings. Trace had been at her side, working with her toward the best possible resolution, and would wonders never cease, he'd actually treated her with respect and, dare she think it, admiration.

Yep, that's what it was. She'd seen it in his expression and in the way he deferred to her. Wow, that had been something.

It wasn't that she was completely unused to being

treated that way. Everyone who worked at the hotel or had had direct dealings with her eventually got that she wasn't an airhead, and she wasn't drunk. Not even when the meetings took place at parties where the champagne flowed. One thing she could do was hold her liquor. What the press didn't know, in fact what no one knew, was that Piper had a system. She knew exactly how much she could drink before it impaired her judgment, and she never went there. Hadn't for years. She grinned. She wasn't a drunk, she just played one on TV.

It served her purpose. That's all that mattered.

But she didn't want to think about interviews or parties right now. She wanted a shower, a long one, and then it would be dinner and Exhibit A. She'd better make plans with Trace.

Sitting on the edge of the bed, she let her hand trail over the silken bedspread. Her phone was in her purse, and her purse was right there, but her thoughts had crawled between the sheets, right back to last night.

It had been…memorable. Incredible, actually, and the more incredible it became, the scarier it got.

He still hadn't budged. Not about Hush. But maybe today had given him a little push. Wouldn't it be ironic if it turned out that he sided with her because of her business smarts instead of her body?

Wouldn't happen. Couldn't. But the whole bedroom thing still had a shot. Her only shot.

She grabbed the phone and called his cell. Left a message for him to call in half an hour. Then she headed for the shower to plan tonight's seduction.

12

HE USED THE KEY Piper had given him. "Piper?"

No answer. He walked through the living room, his duffel bag in tow, to the bedroom. Her dress, a bra and a slip of material that were her panties, lay on the bed, but no Piper.

He put his bag down and went to the bathroom. Knocking loudly, he entered to find her sitting at the vanity. She'd wrapped herself in a Turkish towel, and her hair was wet. He stood where he was, basking in the view. Without makeup, sans any of her usual trappings, she was stunning.

She looked at his reflection in the mirror. Her brow rose when she saw that he was wearing jeans. "You didn't call."

"Did I screw up some plans?"

She shook her head. "I thought we'd eat, then go to Exhibit A."

"Great. I have somewhere I want to take you."

She nodded. "Give me a few minutes."

"Okay," he said as he crossed the room. "Can I watch?"

She seemed taken aback by his request. "Sure."

"Great." He pulled out a little stuffed stool from beneath the far side of the vanity. "Tell me about the interview."

She picked up a jar and unscrewed the lid. Taking a dollop of the cream, she applied it to her face, moving her fingers in slow circles. "Nothing much to say except it'll be fabulous for the hotel."

"I suppose he wanted to know about the sex angle?"

She turned to him with a frown. "Yeah, Trace. Tomorrow we're going to shoot a spread of me using all the toys from the armoire. We'll make a video and give it to the first twenty guests."

"I thought that was reserved for your interview with *Hustler*."

"Did anyone tell you you've got a one-track mind?"

"Seeing you in that towel isn't helping."

With a flick of her wrist she undid the knot at the top of the towel and let the whole thing drop. "Is that better?"

He didn't answer her. He was too busy staring at her body. It disarmed him to see her like that. Sitting so casually, with her makeup spread like a banquet. As if he was privy to a secret ritual.

She laughed, turned back to the mirror and picked up another potion.

He, of course, could pound nails with his dick. Which wasn't part of the plan. Of course they could skip dinner and he could ravish her right here against the shower door, but no, he had plans.

Clearing his throat, he stood up and went for the door, adjusting his jeans as he did so.

Which reminded him. "I'll meet you at the bar," he said. "Dress casually."

"How casually?"

"Remember those torn jeans you told me about?"

She didn't respond, and he didn't dare wait. He hoped that by the time he hit the lobby, his predicament wouldn't be quite so obvious. Or so uncomfortable.

As soon as Trace left, Piper wrapped the towel around herself. It had felt weird being so naked in front of him, and she chastised herself for her foolishness. It was just that kind of stunt that had made the press paint her the slut. While she'd been mortified by the label in her early years, by now it had become her way of flipping the bird at the world.

They were going to think whatever they wanted, and it wouldn't have mattered if she were the most discreet woman on earth, she'd been branded. She'd stopped fighting by the age of nineteen, and just lived her life the way she wanted to.

And while it had been fun to see Trace's reaction, she now wished she hadn't. She wasn't even sure why. Just…

Maybe because it had been so exciting to work with him today. He was so bright, and they'd worked together as if they'd been a team forever. It was the most fun she'd had in a long, long time.

Out of bed, that is.

In bed, being with Trace was just as thrilling. He read her there just as he read her in the boardroom. Why was that?

They were so very different. He couldn't even see the one thing that was most important to her. And yet…

She concentrated on her face, putting on her makeup carefully, as she always did, and wondered what he wanted to do that required torn jeans.

ESCHEWING THE LIMO Piper had on call, Trace hailed a cab on Madison and told the driver to head over to Central Park. It was almost six-thirty when they arrived. A glorious April evening, the park was teeming with skaters and joggers and folks walking their dogs.

Piper adored the park, had grown up here. She'd spent her childhood at the model boat pond, taking gondola rides, watching the polar bears at the zoo. She knew the park, all the secret spots and the hidden nooks. And right now, Trace was taking her to one area she rarely frequented.

"I don't know how to skate," she said, as they reached the rental booth.

"I'll teach you."

She wasn't sure about this, although she had to admit it looked like fun. There was the regular path, where those out for a casual ride could take it slow and easy. Then there was the lane for the speed skaters, which she wouldn't be going near. And then there was the dancer's arena, where talented people did amazing things without falling on their asses.

"What's your shoe size?"

"Eight," she said, then tried to decide if she should be insulted or pleased when he ordered knee pads, shoulder pads and a helmet.

When he handed her the gear, she looked at the black

helmet dubiously. "How worried should I be about where this has been?"

He turned back to the craggy man behind the booth. "How often do you clean those?"

He pointed to a sign. It declared that all helmets and skates were steam-cleaned after each use.

"Okay then," she said, and followed him to a bench.

He had his own skates, which were tons cooler than hers, and his own pads and helmet. When he stood, all decked out, she whistled. And she wasn't kidding. "You look hot."

He laughed. "I look like an overgrown geek."

"But in a sexy way."

He continued to grin. "Make sure the skates are tight. You don't want wobbly ankles."

"That's for sure."

He checked them, then helped her position her pads. She'd worn her jeans, as requested, and one of her favorite shirts. It wasn't much more than a couple of scarves sewn together, but the scarves were Hermés and the print was fabulous, and basically, it made her feel pretty. Of course she'd never accessorized with padding.

"Ready?"

She put her helmet on, tightened the chin strap and said, "As I'll ever be."

He held out his hand, which she took, and she stood.

So far it wasn't nearly as bad as she'd feared. Kind of like ice skates. Why hadn't she done this before?

"The most important thing to know is how to stop,"

Trace said. "'Cause unlike Venice Beach, if you fall here, it's concrete."

"Then I won't fall."

"That's the spirit."

He continued to hold her as they made their way to the slow concourse. He was steady as a rock, but he didn't try to hurry her. Even when little kids whizzed by making rude comments.

She caught him giving wistful glances at the speed lane. "You're really good at this, aren't you?"

"Not especially."

"Liar. I bet you skate like a demon, and God forgive the man, woman or child who gets in your way."

"Where do you get this stuff?" he said, sounding way too offended. "I'm a pussycat."

"My ass," she said.

He cupped the very spot. "And such a pretty one."

"Oh, please!"

He pulled her to a stop. "You want to do this?"

"Yes."

"Watch and learn."

For the next ten minutes, they concentrated on braking. He made her repeat the move until she was ready to kill him, and finally he nodded his approval.

"Can we go now, Teach? Huh, can we?"

He took off before she was the least prepared, turned around to skate backward, and said, "What ya waitin' for?"

She took off after him, swearing revenge, while he

quite literally skated circles around her, but she didn't care because he was laughing like a kid, and she was happy.

And so was Trace, and God, it made all the difference. In all the years she'd known him, she'd never seen him like this. Even the way he laughed was different.

They worked out a rhythm that wasn't too fast for her, and for twenty glorious minutes, they simply skated. People passed them, boom boxes screamed music, Frisbees flew by, and all of it was perfect.

"Over there," he said, pointing to a push cart parked underneath a huge tree.

They made their way to the side of the lane to a hot-dog cart.

"Best in the city," Trace said.

"I haven't had a hot dog in years."

"That can't be good for you."

She laughed. He ordered two for each of them, but she passed on the sauerkraut. They both got bottles of soda, and then they found an empty spot on the grass to dine.

She folded herself into a sitting position where the skates didn't bother her, and so did he. Then they ate in companionable silence, still grinning, still enjoying this rare calm as the day waned.

Just as she was finishing her last bite, she felt a tap on her back. Turning, she saw a young girl, flanked by six of her friends. "Can I have your autograph?"

Piper smiled, but she knew it was over. Just like that. She'd been blessedly anonymous, free to enjoy Trace and the experience, and now she had to be Piper Devon again. It was hard not to let her disappointment show as she signed the girl's backpack.

Trace stood, helped her to her feet, but by the time he'd tossed their trash, there was a full-fledged crowd.

She signed everything from caps to skates to skin, and answered as many inane questions as she could, all the while inching back to the skate lanes.

Trace didn't even try to hide his displeasure, but she couldn't make a clean getaway until she'd made an effort.

He probably didn't realize how ugly something like this could get. He'd never had his hair nearly pulled out at the roots, his clothes torn. Never been spit on. Piper never underestimated the power of a mob.

"Hey, Piper."

She looked up into the face of a guy with greasy hair and a nose ring, who proceeded to tell her how he'd like to go to her sex hotel and see the sights. Only the way he said it made her stomach crawl.

"Okay, that's it."

She felt Trace's hand on her shoulder pull her back, away from the center of the crowd. They didn't make their escape until several more rough male voices made viciously lewd suggestions.

Her spirits plummeted as they headed back, skating now with angry strides, the distance between herself and Trace a gaping chasm.

She could feel his anger, and it mixed with her own. It had been going so well.

They made it to the rental booth without a word

being spoken, and when Trace had returned their gear, he sat on a separate bench to put his shoes back on.

"Trace."

He didn't look at her.

"Trace, they were disgusting morons. Don't let them get to you."

He stood up, although he didn't come nearer. "Is this really what you want? Is this how you want people to think of you?"

"No, of course not. And most people don't."

"One person is too many."

She stood up, and her anger at the men in the crowd was nothing compared to her fury at Trace. "So I'm supposed to live my life according to some uneducated pervert in the street?"

"No, you're supposed to have respect for the Devon name. For yourself."

"You can go straight to hell, Winslow. Don't let the door hit you on the ass."

She walked away, shaking with fury. Who did he think he was? The arbiter of good taste?

It wasn't her fault that some people had no concept of the beauty of sexuality, that they lived and died in the gutter. It didn't mean she was going to change who she was. And if Trace was so offended, it just meant he was more like those creeps than he wanted to acknowledge.

She caught a cab and returned to the hotel. There was still work to be done. And now that her deal with Trace was over, she had to come up with a new strategy. One that might just include the fact that she would no longer be part of the Devon empire.

HE DIDN'T GO back to the hotel. Instead, he caught a cab to his apartment where he cranked up some music as he poured himself a drink.

He couldn't shake his anger at that street scene. He'd wanted to kill that smarmy bastard, wipe him out for having the temerity to be in the same state as Piper.

Dammit, couldn't she see what she was doing? Putting herself out there to be ridiculed and denigrated?

It was worse now. Now that he saw how she could be. Who she was when it stopped being a game.

Even if she was right, and her target clients didn't see the hotel as something tawdry, what about the rest of the world?

Sex was well and fine, but it wasn't the way to market a hotel. Not her hotel. Not her.

If that little demonstration hadn't proved his point, he didn't know what would.

When she'd cooled down, when they both had, he'd talk to her again. Calmly. He'd do whatever he could to help her change the image of Hush. And if she wouldn't? There was nothing left to say.

13

TONIGHT WAS the final run-through. Saturday night Exhibit A would make its debut at the opening-night party. Major celebrities were flying in from Hollywood, from Miami, from all over the world to be here, and to be among the first guests to stay at Hush.

Everything felt like it was happening too fast. Knowing the opening was just days away, suddenly Piper was overwhelmed by the urge to retreat, to hole herself up in her apartment and think. The events at the park kept spinning inside her head, and not just the last part of it. It had been so incredibly normal and wonderful to do something as simple as skate with Trace.

He'd been a revelation. Free, easy, casual. He'd seemed years younger, his ever-present tight control left behind with his shoes.

There had a been a minute there when she'd been filled with a new possibility. That maybe there was more to Trace than she'd ever imagined, and more to what the two of them could mean to each other.

She'd actually felt like she'd been her true self on that skate path. The self she'd almost forgotten existed.

Of course, her illusions had shattered the moment Trace overreacted to that cretin. Trace was Trace, and a quick skate wasn't going to change a thing.

He didn't get it about Hush. He didn't get it about her.

She walked down the narrow white hallway past the black Exhibit A deco sign, pushed open the door and stepped into cool air, dim blue lights and, ah, the smoke. She'd been very skeptical when first approached about using the smoke machine, because in her experience artificial smoke was really stinky. But she'd been assured that the technology had changed, and that this smoke would not only create a mystical atmosphere, but it would scent the air with a hint of mint.

Piper breathed deeply, and there it was. Really faint, but there. Oddly enticing.

The music wasn't loud like at a club, but it was all-encompassing from the ceiling, the floor, the walls. It crawled into her head and found the rhythm of her pulse. Whoa.

Banquettes and tables lined the walls, all facing the center stage, all with high curving sides that gave each setting an atmosphere of intimate privacy. When a couple sat at any table, they would be cocooned, and while they would be able to see the stage, no one would be able to see them. At least the parts below the waist.

She nodded at Eddie, who looked like he could use a drink. The performance hadn't started yet, and still the room worked. Which was important, because the dancers couldn't dance all the time. The atmosphere was infused with mystery. The music combined with the blue lights drifting over the primarily white space made the bar both soothing and exciting.

"Piper."

She turned to see Janice Foster and Mick. Janice scooted over and waved at her to sit with them. She did, wanting to see the room from all perspectives. This was a good place to start.

Besides, she liked them both so much. They'd found each other here, in Hush, and while their relationship had begun in the bedroom it had evolved into full-fledged love. She'd just learned that they were going to be married next fall.

It occurred to her as she scooted into the banquette, that Hush had worked its magic even then. Janice had confided how she'd been so attracted to Mick, but thought anything between them was out of the question. He was so much younger than her, and at first, she couldn't believe he could want her.

But then, as they both let themselves experience Hush, their inhibitions had disappeared and they'd become lovers. "Tell me something," she said, wanting answers from them both. "Why do you believe in Hush?"

"What do you mean?" Janice asked.

"The concept of Hush. I know you love it, and that you're proud of working here. Why?"

"Well, aside from the fact that it's where I met Mick, I believe in the freedom here. The permission to be yourself, to make peace with your sexuality."

Mick nodded. "I felt it. I still do."

"What?" Piper asked, leaning in to hear him better over the music. "What do you feel?"

"Uninhibited. I can be with Janice the way I want to be. It's the only place outside of our place that I can be. We can touch here. Be affectionate."

"Be sexy," Janice said, touching his hand.

"And it's all okay. In fact, it feels kind of weird to hold back." He smiled at Piper. "People should have a place like this. Where they can be as wild as they want to be. Where the regular rules don't apply, and still feel completely safe. It's good for them. There's so much repression out there, where everyone tells you what's right and wrong, about what's acceptable. Hush keeps all that outside the doors, and I'm telling you, it can set people free."

Piper nodded. "I agree. I think it's healthy, but evidently, not all folks do. You don't think it's tawdry, do you?"

Janice laughed. "God, no. It's wonderful. Piper, what's going on? Is it the press?"

She shook her head. "Just taking an informal survey."

"But you researched the hell out of this concept. It's genius. You're not going to be able to keep people away."

"I know. It's gonna be great."

The music changed and smoke built around the circular platform in the middle of the room. As they watched, the platform split, and from the center she watched a couple rise from below as if by magic.

Light and smoke swirled around them, but it was easy to see that they were almost naked. Pressed together, it was their backs she could see, exquisitely toned flesh. They were both tall and lean and beautiful, both from the worlds of ballet and jazz, and they were one of three pairs of dancers who would rotate on the center stage.

As soon as they were completely visible, they stepped lightly to the side of the platform. The silent mechanics closed the trapdoor, leaving them on stage. Piper doubted anyone would notice. They'd be too busy looking at the stunning pair.

They each had on a white G-string. Nothing else.

They posed facing each other, and the dance began. Lifting their arms, they swayed around each other, not quite touching, but almost, skimming just above the flesh, a heartbeat's distance, creating a breathless anticipation. Piper watched them sway to the music. It was as erotic and sensual a sight as she'd ever seen, and she knew right then that Exhibit A would be packed nightly.

Of course, it helped that while the audience watched the show, they could participate with each other. It would take an iron will not to touch, not to want contact when watching the dance.

She leaned back, sneaking a peek at Janice and Mick, who had moved close together. Mick's hand was on Janice's thigh, inching up.

Just as Piper was about to make her excuses and move to another table, the hairs on the back of her neck stood up. She turned, and suddenly there wasn't enough air. It wasn't the smoke, or even the dance. It was Trace.

"Piper."

She couldn't believe he was here. After this afternoon…

"Can we talk?"

She wondered how long he'd been here. Had he heard Janice and Mick? "I don't know. Can we?"

He closed his eyes. His tension was palpable. When he looked at her again, his gaze was pleading.

She turned to the couple next to her. "Have fun, you guys. I'll see you later."

"Okay, Piper," Janice said. "Don't worry, okay?"

She smiled. "I'll do my best." She stood, faced Trace. "Well?"

"Come on. Let's get out of here."

"I have to stay, Trace. People are counting on me."

"Fine." He held out his hand, but she didn't take it. Instead, she led him to a table close to the bar. On her way she saw a lot of employees, including Lisa, sitting by herself, staring at the dancers. But it was Trace who held Piper's attention.

He'd changed from his jeans into dark slacks, a dark silky shirt and a tailored sports jacket. He looked like the epitome of cool grace, someone who'd never find himself eating a hot dog on the grass in Central Park.

She got into the booth ahead of him, searching as she did for the cocktail waitress. The outfits they'd picked for Exhibit A were wonderful in action, and very sixties, all the way from the blue-and-white patterned mini-dresses, to the white go-go boots.

"This is some bar," Trace said, his voice as tense as his posture.

"Thank you."

"At least the costumes won't put you over budget."

She sighed. "I don't need another lecture on standards and morals. Thanks anyway."

The waitress arrived at the table. She smiled at Piper. "Hi, I'm Jessie. What can I get you?"

"Scotch on the rocks," she said. "Make it a double."

"And for you, sir?"

"Vodka on the rocks, Stoli."

"I'll be right back."

Piper didn't say anything, just watched as Jessie headed to the bar.

The music changed and Piper turned to the dancers. It was a much faster beat, dark and sensual, as was the dance itself. The woman raised her arms and fell back, but the man was there to catch her, and when he leaned over her, his lips almost touched her. Moments passed, and Piper wanted them to do it. Kiss, feel, touch. Connect.

Or maybe it wasn't the dancers she wanted to make that final move. She looked at Trace and wondered for the hundredth time what had happened this afternoon. It had begun so well.

He was also staring at the dancers. His lips had parted slightly and she could see the rapid rise and fall of his chest. He was caught in the moment, wrapped in the spell.

She moved closer to him, close enough that she could whisper right in his ear. "Let it happen, Trace. Just feel. Don't think."

Trace wanted to blink, but his eyes wouldn't cooperate. Neither would the rest of him. He watched the tableau in front of him, mesmerized as the couple made love in the center of the room. Okay, so they weren't actually screwing, but they might as well have been. Two little slips of cloth couldn't disguise that this was mating, it was sex.

Piper could call it dancing all she wanted, but it was more than that. The rhythm, the smoke, the lights. It was a scene from a bacchanal, and as much as he'd like to say it was offensive, it wasn't.

It was…hot.

God, it was hard to sit still, hard not to reach over and touch her. He was unbelievably aware of Piper's proximity. Her whisper had gone right through him, twisted in his gut and made his cock come to life. Which wasn't what he'd wanted. Not right now.

He needed to talk to her. To convince her that it was now or never. She had so little time left.

He thought about what he'd overheard Janice and her friend say. How Hush was a place for freedom, for abandon. Of all the things he'd seen at the hotel, this bar had done the most to convince him that there was at least something to that.

It didn't change things. Not really. That the dancers were incredible, that the whole place was something out of an erotic dream would only fuel her father's case.

Although, as he watched, as his body thrummed with an unfamiliar cadence, he wanted to do just what Piper had asked of him. Let go. Stop thinking. Just feel.

Slowly, he turned to look at her. The lights danced across her face, turning her blond hair blue for just a moment, then back to pale. Her lips glistened and her eyes seemed dark and mysterious.

"Do you feel that?" she asked.

He nodded.

She touched his arm and he felt an almost electric shock at the contact. "That's Hush, Trace. Right here, right now. You're in it. And it's not wicked. It's human. It's real."

He shook his head, trying to move his hand, to get some distance. Instead he found himself leaning toward her, wanting to taste her.

The cocktail waitress saved him. She came by with their drinks, then handed him a small card. He had to laugh when he read it. It said Do Not Disturb. "What's this?"

Piper sipped her drink. "It lets the waitresses know that refills aren't necessary. That the couple at the table want privacy."

"So they can what?"

"Participate."

"What does that mean?"

"No one can see what's going on beneath the tables, Trace. It's private. It's for couples. For lovers."

"Unlimited groping? Blow jobs? What?"

Her lips came together in a hard line. "What did you want to talk about?"

He looked away, cursed under his breath. Then he took a drink. After a few seconds, he was ready to face her again. "I'm sorry. I didn't want to go there."

"You never leave there."

"Fine, I'm a shit for wanting to help you. I'm a creep

for wanting to smash that guy's face in. And I must be the worst piece of crap ever for thinking you're more than just sex."

Her expression shifted, although in the damn blue light he couldn't read her. "First of all, I'm a big girl, and I can take care of myself. I don't need your help."

"You don't?"

"No, I don't. I've managed all this time without you taking my bullets."

"That's not what you said the other night. Or wasn't that you telling me that I could have you if only I'd—"

"That was supposed to be quid pro quo. You actually work with me, without prejudice, and I…"

"You what?"

"Never mind. It was a stupid idea, and it's over now, so let's just forget it."

"What do you mean it's over? You still have three days left, or is your pride actually worth half-a-billion dollars?"

She leaned closer to him, and now he could read her like a book. Her anger came off her in waves, and if she could have killed him with a look alone, he'd have been dust. "What. Do. You. Want?"

"You don't believe me when I tell you. But I'll say it again. I want to make this work. I want you to win. I want you and your father to make nice. I don't see how I can be any clearer."

"And the only way you can possibly conceive of this outcome is if I abandon my beliefs? If I toss the whole concept of Hush and become a carbon copy of Daddy?"

"Wait, did I miss the meeting where you came up with a compromise?"

"Dammit, Trace, you come at me like I'm spitting on the family name, and I'm supposed to be thrilled? God, I wish you'd come into the bar five minutes earlier."

"I heard them."

"And what they said meant nothing to you?"

He leaned back, wishing they could leave this music, this pulsing beat that kept intruding on his anger. He kept seeing the dancers in his peripheral vision, and every time, he reacted. It was ridiculous. "I never said you had to abandon everything."

"Oh? What would you have me omit?"

"The PR campaign, for starters."

"Excuse me?"

"Piper, you're in bed. Naked. Looking like you've just been—"

"I know what the ads look like, Trace. I'm in them. And I'm not naked."

"But it's you. Why? Couldn't you have hired a damn model?"

"I'm famous, Trace, and you know what I'm famous for? Nothing. I've done nothing all my life, and I'm the fourth-most-photographed person in the world. There isn't a soul in America, hell, most of the world that doesn't already see me as naked whether I'm dressed or not. The images are there. Always. Hundreds of them, thousands of them, and finally, I'm using them for something besides lining my cat litter."

"Piper, they didn't manipulate those photographs."

She exhaled, then closed her eyes. When she opened them again, she was trembling. "No, they were all me. Every one of them. You're right. I'm exactly what the tabloids say. I'm a ditzy, drunken slut of an heiress who does nothing but screw, party and shop."

"I'm not saying they didn't distort things."

"Distort things? The press? How could you even think that?"

"All right, so you've had more than your share of intrusions in your life. It's not as if you've tried to change your image."

She smiled at him, and it was as cold as the ice in his vodka. "I think I've seen enough to know that Exhibit A is going to be a smashing success. People will line up for blocks. I wouldn't change a thing." She gathered her small purse and stood up.

"Don't go. This isn't over."

She turned to leave, but he caught her wrist. He rose up next to her, close. "I meant to tell you how impressed I was with you this afternoon. You handled the negotiations like a pro."

"Gee, thanks."

"We don't see things the same way, but that doesn't mean I'm inflexible."

She spun on him, getting right up into his face. "You're the most inflexible man I've ever met. You're worse than my father, because at least, if there's enough money involved, he'll bend. It's all a matter of perspective, Trace. We're both watching the same dancers, and where I see beauty and art and sensuality, you see naked tits. You're the one with your mind in the gutter, Winslow. If you think Hush is sleazy, it's because you're bringing sleazy to the party."

She shook her hand free, and walked away. His gaze moved down her body, down the tight dress and the long legs and the sway of her hips.

"Shit." He thought about going after her, but finishing his drink was far more appealing given his state of mind, and hers. His gaze went to the dancers once again. And as the smoke swirled and the beat pulsed in his veins, he thought about what she'd said.

14

MEMORANDUM
To: Staff
From: Janice Foster, General Manager, HUSH Hotel
Date: Thursday
Re: Housekeeping Staff Tutorial
All housekeeping staff please report to conference room A at 9:30 a.m. to go over the guest preferences computer system.

To: Clarissa
Please make sure to put several bouquets in Ms. Devon's suite and office. TREAD SOFTLY!

To: Eddie
Congratulations on Exhibit A! Saturday night, here we come!!!

To: All Staff
Final reports on state of the hotel due tomorrow at 6:00 p.m. NO EXCEPTIONS.

EARTHA KITTY was in heaven. The cat stood quite still for a second, then her whole sleek little body shivered before she skittered off to explore this new territory.

Piper smiled as she watched the black fur ball slinking and stalking and sniffing her way down the first aisle of the rooftop garden. At least something was good. Actually, the garden was good, too, and one of her favorite places in the city. All due to the loving tender care of Clarissa Armstrong, who was one of her favorite people, so it all made sense in a holistic sort of way.

Clarissa, who was in her seventies, lived for this garden. Rows and rows of gorgeous flowers, organic vegetables and hidden secrets. There were columns and railings and pergolas, each of them containing something magical. A plaster frog here, a whirligig there, ideal places to sit, to listen, to smell the orgasmic scents. And there were fountains, too, beautiful little trickling whimsies that soothed the savage beast. And her beast needed soothing today.

She thought about sitting on the bower swing, but chose instead a lovely little stone bench where she could keep an eye on Eartha. Twenty minutes. That's all she had to savor this idle pursuit. To stop and quite literally smell the flowers. No thoughts of work, of Trace, of Nicholas, of unions of anything but sunshine and sweetness were going to intrude. She'd spent the whole night tossing and turning, not sleeping, hating life, hating Trace, hating most everything, and she needed a break.

Eartha pounced on something. Piper wished she'd brought her video camera because it was just so damn cute. Water trickled softly nearby as she watched the grand battle: Eartha versus broken petal. The petal didn't stand a chance.

"Well, hello."

Piper turned at Clarissa's voice. "Morning."

"It's nice to see you. It's been too long."

Clarissa looked wonderful, as always. Her hair looked youthful even though it was a perfect white, maybe because of the curls. Like Shirley Temple only not dorky. Today she had on green slacks and a white blouse. She looked like spring. "It has been too long. The garden is fabulous."

"It is. But come Saturday, people will come. People who leave empty cups and step off the path."

"We'll have surveillance cameras mounted immediately, and all litterbugs will be shot."

"I appreciate the gesture. Now would you like to continue to commune with the cat, or would you like to talk?"

"Talk would be good."

Clarissa sat, folding one long leg over the other. "Pardon the observation, but you don't look very happy. Is the hotel not ready?"

"It'll be ready. Not completely, because that would be a miracle, but close. Enough to open."

"Ah, so if it's not the hotel…?"

"Would you like Hush if it was, say, a different kind of hotel?"

"I'm not sure I understand."

"What if it wasn't the sexiest hotel to ever exist in

Manhattan? If it was a Devon hotel. You've stayed at a Devon hotel, right?"

The older woman nodded. "I have. I've stayed at the Orpheus and at several of the smaller hotels. One in San Francisco and one in Hawaii."

"So?"

"I'm still not entirely sure what you're asking me."

"Okay." Piper took in some more of the glorious air. "What if Exhibit A was just a regular bar? With no dancers at all. And if the rooms didn't have naughty videos or toys or the *Kama Sutra* in the drawers? What if the ads on all the billboards and in the magazines had pictures of the lobby or, I don't know, the pool and spa? If it wasn't Hush, would you still like it here? Would you think it was special?"

Clarissa didn't answer for a long time. Long enough for Piper's thoughts to spiral down and down.

"Although it wouldn't exactly be Hush," she said, finally, "it would still be a wondrous hotel. The guests would still come."

"What guests?"

"All kinds."

"Why?"

"Piper, the hotel is elegant and comfortable and absolutely stunning." Clarissa reached over and touched Piper's hand. "And they would still make love, they'd still find romance." She spread her arms to encompass the rooftop. "Who could resist cupid's arrow in a garden this lovely? The sheets will still be sinfully soft, and the bathtubs will still hold couples. I don't think you could stop people from understanding the true heart of Hush if you tried. Not even if you called it Devon's Bastard Hotel and Inn."

Piper smiled. Her head wanted to deny Clarissa's words, but she couldn't. It wasn't as if what Clarissa had said was bad. She had built the hotel for love, and not just because of the toys. Every design feature was made to evoke emotion, to free the inhibitions. But dammit, she didn't want to take away the toys. The toys were cool and fun and she'd put a lot of thought and care into picking them out.

"I must attend to my roots," Clarissa said. "But please come visit more often. The garden is so much more alive when you're here."

"Thank you."

"Nonsense." The older woman stood. "Don't forget kitty."

Piper didn't actually see the cat, and so she went in search. She found her on her back, batting a morning glory. Piper lifted her into her arms and scratched the black tummy as she walked slowly toward the elevator.

"ANGELA, I'M GLAD you're in so early. I need some things." Trace finished wiping the shaving cream off his chin, then headed for the bedroom, his cell phone still up to his ear. "All the files on market research. Everything."

"It's a lot of files."

"I know. But I'd appreciate seeing it all."

"No problem."

"Thanks. I'll be in my room." He hung up, then dialed room service, which, he was happy to say, was up to speed. He ordered eggs, wheat toast, orange juice and a large pot of coffee. Yeah, he had the small pot furnished by the hotel, but frankly, he didn't want to bother. Once that was done, he opened the drapes halfway so the glare wouldn't affect his computer screen, then he tackled his e-mail.

He didn't give himself a minute. He'd done enough thinking. Now it was time for action.

Piper's discourse last night hadn't gone down well. He'd been awake until about three as he tried to put aside his prejudices and look at the hotel from her perspective.

He still wasn't convinced that she was right, but he was determined to give her the benefit of the doubt. At least for the next couple of days, he would be open to all possibilities. Everything, including Piper's approach to Hush, was entirely appropriate.

His cell rang, and he checked his watch. It was eight forty-five, and that could only mean one thing. "Hello, Nicholas."

"I haven't heard from you."

"I have nothing new to report."

"And why is that?"

"We're working things out."

"There's a new billboard on Broadway. Piper looks like she's inviting the Seventh Fleet into her bed."

"I'm working on it."

"I want the billboard replaced."

"I'll talk to her."

"You know full well that talking to Piper is futile."

"It's still her hotel."

"Remind her again how much she stands to lose."

Trace held back his sigh. This was his boss. His job. His only source of income. "Is there anything else?"

"There are naked dancers in the downstairs bar."

"They're not naked. Not completely."

"Trace."

"I was there, Nicholas. It was very tasteful."

"It won't sound tasteful in the papers. This has to stop. Have you read today's *Wall Street Journal?*"

"Not yet."

"Read page eight and tell me again how tasteful things are."

"I'll call you, Nicholas."

The man hung up. Trace turned off his own phone and thrust the conversation out of his mind. He was not going to change his plans.

At EIGHT-FIFTEEN, Piper was finally done. She'd spent the morning in the screening room, and it was everything she'd wanted it to be. It wasn't large, just big enough for executives to see dailies, or have private viewings. Twenty of the most comfortable chairs on earth, bar service, room service, and even popcorn, the real fresh-popped kind.

After that, she'd met with Janice, and then she and Kit had spent several hours going over the opening night party, among other things. She'd grabbed some food in the employees' cafeteria, had way too much coffee, and generally, aside from the few moments in the garden, it had been one hell of a tough day.

She got off the elevator and put the key card in the lock upside down. Twice. Finally, she walked inside and heard music.

She hadn't left music on this morning. All of the guests had the option of having housekeeping turn on the stereo, but she hadn't requested that. And there was a new floral arrangement on the coffee table, and what was that scent?

She knew this was her suite, at least until next Monday, so why was she hearing footsteps?

Trace.

She hadn't seen him all day. At four, she'd called down to the front desk to see if he'd checked out. He hadn't. But he hadn't called her, either, and she'd assumed he'd taken her at her word last night and gone back to the Orpheus to tell Nicholas to change the will.

Now he was standing in her bedroom door.

"I'm tired, Trace. I've had a really long day, and all I want to do is take a bath and go to sleep. So if you want to argue with me, can you do it in your own room? I promise to argue back first thing tomorrow."

"Piper," he said, walking right for her. "Shut up."

"Excuse me?"

He moved behind her and put his hands on her shoulders. As he urged her forward he leaned close to her ear and whispered, "No arguing. No witty comebacks. No talking whatsoever."

"Trace."

"Uh-uh. What did I just say?" He pushed her into her bedroom, and there was her big white fluffy Turkish robe on the bed. "Take off your clothes."

"Trace—"

"If you don't take off your clothes, I'll take off your clothes, which isn't a horrible idea except that it's not on the agenda. So shut up and take off your clothes."

"What the hell are you doing?" She turned to face him. "And why are you looking so smug?"

"All your questions will be answered the moment you're naked."

"I've had that seminar before, and no thanks."

"Oh, ye of little faith."

She laughed. "I'm supposed to trust you?"

"Yes, you are."

"Based on what?"

"Based on the fact that it would drive you insane not to get to the bottom of this."

"If I had even one ounce of energy, I'd hurt you."

"Then you'd probably be wiser to stop stalling and get naked."

"Are you going to stand there and watch?"

His brows came down for a moment. "No. That's not on the agenda, either. I'll be in there." He pointed to the bathroom.

"Are you going to run me a bath?"

"No more questions."

"Oh, God, all right. Just go. I promise I'll strip, I'll do anything, if you'll just go away."

He smiled brilliantly and walked into her bathroom.

She stared at the empty door for a minute, and then she gave in. She wasn't going to sleep with him, no matter how charming he thought he was being. Even if he poured her a bath and scrubbed her back, he was out of here. What, did he think this made up for everything? That she'd forget his words, his obstinacy?

She dropped her dress right where she stood, then took off her bra and panties. Her shoes came off at the same time, and she wrapped herself up in the big robe. She would have done this anyway, so it didn't matter that he was still in the bathroom. Although she didn't hear the water running, so what was he doing?

Padding across the smooth wood floor she felt the beginnings of a headache forming at the base of her skull as she went in search of Trace. She'd kick him out, then get on with her night. Not on the agenda. Who did he think he was?

She stopped and stared.

Caroline. What's-her-name, the newest masseuse. Two massage tables. Eucalyptus and freesia. Oh.

"Surprise."

Trace was in his robe, too, which was interesting, because she didn't remember having a robe for him in her suite. And where the heck had he undressed? "What's all this?"

"Massage."

"Thanks, I figured that part out for myself."

Caroline walked over to her, smiling soothingly. "It's been a rough week, Piper. Let's get you on the table."

"Thanks, Caroline, but there's been a little mistake."

"No, there hasn't," Trace said. "No mistake at all. This is part of me understanding Hush."

"We've been over this."

"And you were right."

She blinked. "Pardon me?"

"I've been narrow-minded. I haven't given the hotel a chance. That changes now."

"With a couples' massage."

"Right."

"And then?"

"And then, you sleep. Tomorrow, we talk."

"Who are you, and what have you done with Trace?"

He sighed. "I don't know about you, but my back is killing me. And what do you know, there are two professional masseuses right here ready to take away the pain."

The headache was getting worse. The tables were already set up, and there was the hotpot with the scented oil, and the music was Delibes… "I won't get rid of you any other way, will I?"

He shook his head.

"Fine."

Caroline put her arm around Piper's shoulders and led her to the far table. She held up the sheet while Piper took off her robe, then gently covered her as she lay down on her stomach. The table was covered with another sheet, but this one was warm.

Her eyes closed as soon as she was flat. She heard Trace settling next to her, close enough that if they reached out at the same time, they could hold hands. Of course, she wasn't going to reach for him. Not a chance. This could actually be considered research. She was supposed to try all the massages, and she hadn't gotten to couples yet.

Caroline pulled down the sheet to bare her back, and an instant later, warm, oiled hands began their work. Piper moaned at the first touch.

The music, the duet by the two ladies that was her favorite piece in the world, filled her head as bliss filled her body. Even the fact that Trace Winslow was getting equal treatment a foot away couldn't disturb the magic. She moaned again as Caroline manipulated her neck.

Deep breath in, deep breath out. Nothing but calm, soothing breaths.

But the thoughts wouldn't stay away. Thoughts of her meeting with Kit. New campaign concepts. More subdued. Not Devon, but not exactly Hush. Hush quiet. Hush…light.

"Trace?"

"No talking."

"I've been thinking."

"Good for you, but don't think now."

"It's about your wacky compromise idea."

"Tomorrow."

"Trace…"

"Piper!"

"Never mind."

"There you go."

15

PIPER REALIZED somewhat groggily that she wasn't laying on a beach in Cabo. She was still in her suite being pampered and petted like a spoiled kitty. She also realized that the sheet that had been tucked over her butt had disappeared leaving her naked on the table.

She lifted her head a bit. "Caroline?" Her voice came out scratchy and thick.

"Shh."

"But—"

"Hush."

She let her head rest again in its little nest, but something about the whispered word stayed with her. Along with the feeling of the hands running up her thighs.

Big hands. Male hands.

She tensed, and he stilled.

"Relax," he whispered. "It's all right." He touched both her hands with his, then in one long, firm stroke, he moved up her arms, across her shoulders, then down her back. The flow continued down her buttocks to her thighs and her calves. He didn't stop until he'd gone all the way to her toes.

It was an amazing sensation, made more so by the knowledge that it was Trace touching her with such care, such firm strength.

As he worked his way back up her body, her breathing changed along with her awareness. She felt her breasts against the sheet, the warm air between her legs.

His attention shifted to the cheeks of her ass, squeezing the flesh from the crease at her thigh to the base of her back. It was incredibly sexual. Every time he squeezed, her cheeks parted just a bit. And when he moved down to knead her inner thighs, his knuckles brushed her sex.

Piper gasped, no longer in that blissful state of relaxation. "Trace."

"Hush," he said again. "This is what it's about, right?" He bent over her, his warm breath tickling her ear. "I want to make you feel good. In every possible way."

She whimpered as he slipped one finger inside her and stroked, lightly, up and down. "I'm still mad at you."

"I know. You can beat me up later. Now, all I want you to do is let go." He nipped her earlobe and made her shudder, never stopping the intimate rubbing. "You're getting so wet," he said. "So ready."

"Oh, God."

He kissed the back of her neck. "I'll be right back. Don't move."

She couldn't if she wanted to. Every bone in her body had turned to rubber. She felt heavy on the table and all her private parts were begging for more attention.

He didn't keep her waiting long. She heard him before she felt him and even then it wasn't his hands on her skin, but the softest, most tantalizing sensation. Fur. He had gotten the fur gloves from the night table and he was rubbing them all over her back, her legs, her arms.

She moaned again, unable to hold back.

The fur disappeared and a moment later his hands slipped under her side. "Let's turn you over," he said.

She wasn't quite sure she wanted to be on her back. Yeah, she'd been naked with him before, but she felt really exposed. Still, she didn't resist. In fact, she helped, settling herself on the middle of the cushioned table.

Trace hadn't dressed. He was as naked as she was, and he took her breath away. So beautiful, and the way he looked at her made her forget their argument. Almost.

"We keep ending up like this," she said. "But it never changes anything."

"Don't be so sure." He brushed her face lightly with his fingertips. "Will you trust me?"

"Never."

He laughed. "Please? Trust me here. I want to show you something."

She closed her eyes. "Okay."

He leaned over and kissed her, a shuddering brush against her lips which grew deeper as the seconds went by. His tongue slipped inside her, and as he'd done with his finger, he stroked back and forth, a teasing sweetness that made her long for more.

He pulled back instead. "Keep your eyes closed," he said, his voice lowered to that smoky whisper.

His hands were on her wrists, lifting her arms above her head. More fur, only this time it was cuffs, and when he was finished, her movements were restricted—she couldn't lower her hands.

His bare feet on marble, hands on the inside of her thighs, parting them to the edges of the table. Fur cuffs on her ankles, too. Nothing tight, nothing uncomfortable. She could still arch her back, thrust up with her hips, moan with need.

"You're so beautiful," he said. "I could look at you forever."

"More," she said, although if pressed she couldn't have said whether she wanted him to touch her harder or say more pretty things.

He lifted his hands. She waited impatiently, struggling to keep her eyes closed. Every part of her longed for his touch, his caress. What she got was warm, almost hot, oil in a steamy trickle between her breasts, down over her stomach. She almost laughed when it pooled in her belly button, but then she felt the warmth on her mound, dripping between her legs.

He started with a proper massage, moving from top to bottom. Well, not all the way to the bottom. He stalled about three-quarters of the way down. Slick with more than just oil, he did things to her that needed to be added to the *Kama Sutra*.

Piper couldn't keep still. Her hips lifted, she arched her back, she cried, she begged, and he just kept on tormenting her with pleasure just intense enough to keep her *right there* on the edge.

"Come on, baby. You can take it. Just a few more minutes."

"No. Please. Oh, God, please. There, right there."

The table trembled and at first she thought it was from her own shaking, but then she felt his leg move over hers. He stopped touching her.

"Trace, dammit—"

He laughed. "Patience."

"No!"

He lifted her knees with his own, and then his fingers were back and this time, he wasn't fooling around. He found her clitoris and circled it with his thumb. Perfect pressure, perfect tempo, perfect…perfect, and oh, God, her muscles tensed and she came, straining against her bonds as the spasms hit one after the other, spreading through her body.

Before she could even catch her breath, he was inside her. No more hands, at least not there. Just his hard, thick cock, and there was no better feeling, not any massage, not anything in the world that was more intense and perfect than that first thrust.

His low groan told her it wasn't half-bad for him, either. She gasped, pulled at her wrists, needing to touch him. "Please," she said, "undo my hands. Please."

He paused. Nodded. Leaned over her body while still deeply inside her, and unclipped the restraints. The second she was free, she wrapped her arms around his neck. Pulled him down into the kiss she'd been wanting for too long.

HE TURNED OVER SO that he could feel more of her body. Piper still smelled like the floral bath soap from the shower, and he needed to find out what the scent was so he could buy her a case. The smell was intoxicating, making him want her all over again.

But it was too late, and frankly, he was so spent, he wasn't sure he could get it up again. Nah, for her he could. Anytime, anywhere.

But she was all snuggled next to him, and she'd been tired before all the fun and games.

"Trace?"

"Hmm?"

"You said you wanted to show me something."

"Oh, yeah."

"What was it?"

He grinned. "The brand-new me."

She opened one eye. "What?"

"Did you wonder where I was all day?"

"I figured you were telling Dad to change the will."

"Not exactly."

"Okay, then where were you?"

"In my suite. Looking at your market research."

Both eyes were open now. "Oh?"

"You did a good job, Piper."

"I know."

"Well, I didn't. Not until today. You were thorough and meticulous and I couldn't find a stone unturned."

She shifted away, balanced her head on her hand. "And?"

"I can see where the concept of Hush is a timely idea.

There isn't a hotel like it in New York, but there are all kinds of special hotel packages that offer an erotic experience, and from your records, they're doing a fantastic business."

"I know."

"So I can tell Nicholas that the money will come."

"But?"

"There's still the issue of the Devon name."

"Oh, come on, Trace. The Devons can't live in the past forever."

"It's not a question of modernism, Piper. It's image and it's not a joke. The Devon name means a great deal."

"Dammit—"

"Hold on. Just hold on a minute. I don't want you to take this the wrong way, but your father's in his seventies. He won't be around forever. And then—"

"You're kidding, right? He's strong as an ox. He'll outlive the continental shelf."

"He won't. And then you'll be able to do whatever you like. But not if you're disinherited. Is it really worth it? Fighting so hard?"

She let her head drop to the pillow. "I don't know. Maybe it is."

"Hey."

"What?

"Come on, look at me."

She pulled herself up and packed a pillow behind her back. "I'm all attention."

"You said something to me. When you were on the table. About that wacky compromise idea of mine?"

"Oh, that."

"Come on. Out with it."

"I met with Kit. We talked about changing some of the ad campaign."

"Interesting."

"Under no circumstances will I make this into a Devon hotel. Know that right now. I won't."

"Okay. So what are you willing to do?"

"We can talk about it. Tomorrow. I asked Kit to put together some new concepts. We'll look at them. But I'm not promising anything."

"Fair enough. Although, there isn't much time left."

"Believe me, I know."

"Okay. This was good. Very good. So why don't we get some sleep? We'll tackle it all in the morning."

"I set the alarm for five."

He groaned. "That's just wrong."

"So quit touching me."

"I'm not."

"Then what's that on my ass?"

He laughed. "Okay, okay. I'm officially removing my hand from your delectable ass. And I'm closing my eyes."

She sighed. Scooted down under the covers. The quiet was almost total. He could just hear her soft breathing. The slightest snick of silk against silk. Then…

"Piper."

"Hmm?"

"If you continue to touch that, neither of us will get any sleep."

"Sorry."

"It's okay."

"'Night."

"'Night."

"I'LL MEET YOU."

Piper, looking gorgeous in a little black skirt, white blouse, and absurdly high heels, stopped messing with her hair to look at him. "Are you all right?"

"Yeah. Fine."

"You had a bad dream."

"What?"

"You woke me about four. You were calling out."

He felt his face heat up and he turned to the mirror to straighten his tie, hoping she couldn't see him properly. "I don't remember."

"You seemed really upset."

"It was nothing, I'm sure. Probably thinking about my next meeting with your dad."

"Funny. You're a funny guy."

"Go. Eat something decent. You're too skinny."

"Ha." She got her purse and her briefcase, then came to his side. "Last night was…"

He smiled. "I'll say."

"So I'll see you."

He nodded. Then he leaned down and kissed her lips, sorry she'd already put on her lipstick. He liked her au natural, but it wasn't so bad. She still tasted like Piper.

She touched his cheek, then turned and walked out of the bedroom. His smile faded as he heard the outer door close.

He'd been having the dream a lot lately. Probably just the stress of all this. Nicholas. Piper. Once the hotel opened, he'd be fine. He'd stop thinking about what happened. There wasn't a damn thing he could do about it, anyway. Bob was dead. No amount of nightmares would bring him back.

PIPER SAT in her office, her yogurt and fruit untouched as she went through the stack of magazine ads. Of course she'd seen her own ads a hundred times, but she had new eyes this morning. She was looking for context. For shock value. For anything that would help her make some decisions.

She spread them out across the desk, full-page color ads, all of them starring herself. Looking like she needed a good shag. She laughed, looking at the one with the diamond necklace. If only the world knew that what she'd really needed at that particular moment was a corned beef sandwich from the Broadway Deli. She'd been starving, and the photographer had been achingly slow. She hadn't had one thought about sex, and yet, she'd been practicing for the pose most of her life, hadn't she?

She thought again about what Trace had said. That she was responsible for her own image as well as the hotel's. And while she still believed with all her heart that an erotic hotel was a wonderful thing, and that people deserved a place to go and be as hedonistic as they wanted to be, why was she still playing the vixen to the press?

She knew exactly how it had begun. Pictures, innocent pictures, that had been taken without her knowledge. Anyone could have been in her situation. She'd tripped over something in a club. Her blouse had come undone. It wasn't meant to be provocative, and she'd been drinking soda, not booze. But the paper had painted her as trollop of the year. That had been the start. Then, no matter where she went, they all wanted the nasty shot. They crawled on the ground to shoot up her skirt. One photographer had held his camera over her toilet stall. Her life had been hijacked by the tabloids, and it didn't matter in the least that she wasn't the person they lasciviously described.

Her father had been incensed. He blamed her entirely, not even giving her explanation a moment of credence. So she'd made up her mind, if they wanted a slut, she'd give them a slut.

That had been years ago. She'd grown accustomed to it. And with Hush, she'd concluded that as long as that was the way it was, she might as well capitalize on the infamy.

But was it how she wanted it to be forever? Did she want to be forty, and still be seen as the slutty, ditzy heiress? Was it even possible to change the way the world saw her?

Her gaze went back to the photo, to her eyes. Who the hell was that woman? What was she trying to prove?

She'd told him the truth the other night. She was famous for nothing. For winning the genetic lottery, perhaps. Nothing she'd done was noteworthy. She'd made appearances at charities, donated lots of money and even some time, but anyone could do that. The only thing that was hers and hers alone was Hush.

If she changed the campaign, if she made the hotel less about sex, would it still be hers? Would it give her what she needed so badly?

PIPER STEPPED into the lobby and was blindsided by popping flashbulbs. The press had swarmed the hotel, and they were shouting her name. And another name.

"Logan, what about the rest of the tour?"

"Are you here to try out the sex at Hush?"

"Logan, over here!"

Logan? What the hell? He was supposed to be on the road. They'd agreed. She'd told him it was over, and though he'd laughed, she'd thought he understood. So why was he here?

"Hey, baby."

"Logan. What's going on?"

"You thought you could keep me away from the opening of a sex hotel?"

"Why don't we go to my office. We can talk. Privately."

She could smell the liquor on his breath. She doubted, given the glassiness of his eyes, that he was only high on booze. She needed to get him out of here, and away from her.

"Let's give them a little somethin', eh, Piper?" He lurched toward her, his hand grabbing her shoulder.

She jerked back, not wanting him, not wanting this. While he'd been annoying before, now he repulsed her. Everything about what they'd been made her ill.

The flashbulbs blinded her, and the crush of bodies made her heart race. She had to get out of here, away from this insanity.

Another hand, strong, sure, took her by the upper arm, and led her away toward the elevator. Like a leech, Logan held on to her, but she didn't care as long as she could get away from the mob.

She lost her footing once, but she didn't fall. Because Trace held her up. It was Trace in front of her, holding on to her, helping her escape.

She gazed up into his worried eyes, then back at the drunk and stoned Logan.

Millions of women wanted Logan, dreamed of him, would have done anything to be in his bed. And he was nothing compared to Trace. Who made her crazy. Inflexible, demanding, rude. Incredible Trace.

He got them into the elevator and blocked her from the cameras. Piper leaned against the stainless steel wall, gasping hard to refill her lungs. She smiled at Trace when he turned around.

"Jesus, Piper."

He wasn't worried. He was angry. Disgusted.

"No, you don't understand." She shook off Logan's hand. "It's not what you think."

"Is it ever enough?" he said, his voice very low. Then his gaze moved down to her chest.

She looked at her reflection in the door. Her blouse was open, her bra pushed down just enough to expose her right nipple.

They'd gotten it again. The money shot.

16

TRACE GOT OFF on his own floor. Piper had buttoned up her blouse while Logan leered at her. What the hell had she seen in him? Logan was drunk, he smelled, his hair was filthy and his clothes a joke. Trace had always hated his band, hated his voice, hated him. And Piper had invited him to the opening? Nice of her to mention it.

He slammed his suite door shut, too angry and disappointed to sit down. What was it with her? One step forward, two steps back. Couldn't anything be easy?

It was just past noon and they were supposed to meet at three with Kit to go over the ad campaign. As if it would do a damn bit of good. She seemed determined to make Hush the most notorious hotel in New York.

He sat at the desk, opened his laptop, but it was no good. He needed to get out of here for a while. Go for a walk. See something other than this hotel.

It took him almost fifteen minutes to get out. The press was camped out in the lobby. Lisa Scott and Janice Foster were doing everything they could to clear the place, but Trace doubted they had enough security on the premises.

Well, with the big party only a day away, he supposed

it was good publicity—if one subscribed to the belief that any publicity was good.

He headed down Madison, not caring at all where he ended up, just so long as it wasn't Hush. The air was warm, the crowds not too thick. After striding down a couple blocks, he'd finally cooled off.

It just wasn't working, that's all he had to admit. A job gone wrong. Not everything was smooth sailing, and he and Piper...

There was no "he and Piper." He belonged to the job, and she was... She was a force of nature. So he saw more in her. So what? But if she didn't see it herself, what was he supposed to do about it?

Hell, who was he to judge? The woman had a life he could barely comprehend even though he'd been around her most of her life. But who could know what it was like to be followed everywhere? To have no privacy in public. To have her life documented in tabloids, to have each moment captured for better or worse.

She had money and looks and what most people would think was the ideal life. But he knew better. He understood exactly what pressure her father put on her, how he'd hated that his first born was a girl. How hard it had been that she'd lost her mother so young.

No one had it easy, including Piper. But she also had advantages, lots of them.

He walked by a newsstand, and there she was, plastered on three different tabloids. None of the pictures were particularly flattering, but she was at least fully clothed. By tomorrow, that would be different. If only she'd worn a different bra. Everyone walking down this street would see her breast.

He slowed his pace as it hit him that he didn't want anyone seeing Piper undressed. Anyone else.

He cursed Logan, evidently aloud, given the look he got from an older woman carrying her groceries.

Logan, bloody Barrister. Sleaze personified. Trace didn't get it, and he didn't get why he cared so much. It couldn't be just because of their chemistry in bed.

Okay, so that probably had something to do with it. She was terrific, and he'd never...

He walked again, all his hard-fought calm shot to hell. He'd never experienced anything like being with Piper. Of course, he'd never met anyone who frustrated him more, either, when they got together. Damn.

He thought about the massage, how she'd been so incredibly responsive. It had been torture to wait, but all he wanted was to make her go crazy. He'd heard men say that they got turned on by turning their women on, and he'd nodded and smiled and known they were lying through their teeth. He owed them an apology.

His pace slowed once again. She'd been willing to compromise. Not to fold, which honestly, he'd never expected, but she'd offered a branch of hope. They were going to talk about a new campaign. One where she wasn't half-naked. So maybe she'd forgotten about Logan? Or maybe she figured she had to pull out every trick she could?

Piper was scared. Of course she was. She wanted to

have her own success, she wanted something that was hers alone, and he couldn't blame her.

Another newsstand, only this time, a young woman was reading one of the tabloids with Piper on the cover. He approached her, trying not to look like a mugger. "Excuse me."

She looked up. He guessed she was in her twenties, wearing the traditional New York black, her hair stylish, her makeup just right. She gave him a quick once-over, then smiled. "Yes?"

"I don't mean to interrupt, but I'd like to ask you a question. What do you know about Piper Devon?"

She shrugged. "Rich, pampered, great style. Likes to party."

"Have you heard about her hotel?"

"Are you taking a survey?"

"Sort of."

"Yeah, I've heard of it. Can't help it."

"And?"

She closed the paper and put it down, staring at Piper for a moment. "I like it. I think it would be fun to stay there, if I could afford it."

"So you like the concept behind it?"

She smiled at him, and this time her once-over wasn't so quick. "What's not to like? Sex and hotels go together. Only this one is taking it to the next level."

"Okay, thank you. I appreciate your honesty."

"You're welcome." She reached into her large black purse and pulled out a business card. "If you want to do some personal research at Hush, well…"

He took the card. She was an editorial assistant for a publishing company. Elaine Waycroft. "Thanks. I'll let you know." He continued his walk, stuffing the little card into his jacket pocket.

Elaine Waycroft fit the profile for the perfect Hush guest. She didn't make the kind of money to treat herself to the hotel, but she probably dated men who did. Young, single, hip. Piper was right, they would come. There was money to be made and a new clientele to cater to. There would always be room for hotels like the Orpheus, and for the Devon chain, but the times were changing and someone had to be on the front lines.

Of course, it would be Piper. Having to fight every step of the way. She'd done it, though. The tricky part was that on paper, it looked like a strictly business move, but he knew for a fact that her motivation wasn't so pure.

Daddy had made her toe the line every moment she'd lived under his roof. She wasn't a kid anymore, and it was time for her rebellion to end. For her own good.

Somewhere, there had to be a workable solution. If she made a few modifications Piper could have Hush and her inheritance. All he had to do was figure out exactly what would have to change. He no longer believed she should turn the hotel into a Devon. It needed to be Hush. But maybe not quite so Hush.

Compromise, that was the word of the day. If they could talk. If that bastard Logan wasn't there.

And once the hotel issue was solved, once Trace was back on his own home turf, he'd look at the situation between the two of them. If there even was a situation.

"I DIDN'T ASK you to come."

"Surprise."

Piper went over to the window and looked down at the street. There were people walking, cars and taxis, the whole city was alive with bustle and purpose. She'd love to take a walk. A long one. Stopping in stores that caught her eye, maybe a little shopping. Anonymously. Privately. Just another customer, another pedestrian. But she couldn't do that.

She turned to face Logan who was lounging on the chaise. Of course he'd found the liquor, as if he hadn't had enough. "Logan, we're done. We were done a long time ago. I didn't invite you to the party because I don't want you here."

His head lolled back. "Right. You don't want me. That's a laugh, girl."

"Oh, God. Have you been reading *Tiger Beat* again? There are hundreds of groupies waiting to hold your hair back while you vomit. Go find one of them."

"But darlin', it's you and me. We're a match made in heaven. We look marvelous in all those pictures, don't you think?"

"I don't care. I have other things that are more important than getting my picture taken."

He laughed. Really laughed. Then he coughed for a long time. When he could breathe again, he looked at her. "You don't have a life that's not in the tabloids, baby."

"That's it. Out. Go. Where the hell's Martin? He never lets you far off the leash."

"Bloody Martin is with Keith, working on the Madison Square Garden gig."

Piper got her purse, her cell. She found Logan's manager's number in her speed dial and called. "Martin, this is Piper. Can you please come get Logan? He's wasted here at Hush, and I can't have him here."

Martin hesitated. "What? Trouble in paradise?"

"Logan, being the genius he is, doesn't understand the words 'It's over.' I'm hoping you can make him see the light. I don't want him here now, or ever. Certainly not at the party. Can you take care of this?"

"Wait a minute, Piper. Let's think this through. The publicity for both of you would be great."

"I don't care. I want him gone. If you don't do it, I'll be forced to call in the police. With his tox level, I'm thinking you don't particularly want that."

Martin, long used to having to babysit for the boys in the band, sighed. "Give me two hours. I've got to finish up here."

"Two hours, Martin. That's it."

"Yeah. See you, Piper."

She hung up the phone. Logan was still smiling at her, as if it was all a colossal joke. She no longer cared. "I have a meeting," she said. "You, stay here. Drink yourself into a coma for all I care, but don't leave the suite. Martin will be here soon to get you."

He looked at her, suddenly serious. "Piper."

"Yes?"

"You have any almonds? I could really go for some roasted almonds."

She shook her head, got her purse and left. Hoping beyond hope that the press had vacated. She didn't go to the lobby to find out, but straight to her office.

She returned a bunch of phone calls, mostly from publicists of guests. When she could finally breathe again, she simply sat in her chair, staring at the wall. Would Trace show up at the meeting?

Why? Why did he always think the worst? Why didn't he ask? It wasn't fair, and she should be a lot angrier than she was.

If he would just *see* her. But, like everyone else, he was blinded by the lights of the paparazzi. Which she'd expected, so why in hell did it hurt so much? The look on his face had been so disappointed. Disgusted. As if she'd ripped her own blouse just for kicks.

If they'd just had sex, she could understand, but it had been more. They'd talked. Worked through some stuff. But then what did she know? Her track record with men sucked the big one, so why should Trace be different?

Because he was Trace. Because he'd known her forever. Because he should know better.

Oh, well. She'd survive. She still had to get through the next two days. Make decisions about the ad campaign, about Hush. She just had to stop wishing for things that didn't exist.

Funny, up until two hours ago, she hadn't even realized she'd been wishing at all. That somehow Trace had become…something to her. She wasn't even sure what. All she knew for sure is that it wasn't much. How could it be when she disgusted him? When he thought so very little of her?

She picked up the phone, called Kit. Asked her where she was on the new ideas. When she hung up, she thought about all the things she had to do in the hour before the meeting.

She made one more call, up to Trace's suite. He wasn't there.

"HEY, JACE, it's Lisa Scott. From Hush." Lisa sat back in her leather chair, willing her heart to stop beating so hard. It was ridiculous to be this nervous. He was just a guy, and it would come to nothing, so what was her problem?

"Hey, Lisa. I was just going over my notes."

"Did you get everything you needed?"

"From Piper, yeah. But it wouldn't hurt my feelings if you'd sit down with me for an hour or so."

"Me?"

"You're her closest friend."

"True. Which means I don't dish. Ever."

"Not interested in anything but the truth."

"Gee, you're the first journalist who's ever said that to me."

He laughed. "I won't bring my thumbscrews or any other torture devices, I promise."

"Bummer."

He didn't comment, and she cursed her stupid sense of humor.

"I think this is going to be a fun interview," he said, finally. "So when can we meet?"

"Tonight? Say, eight? I could get us in to Amuse Bouche. I have connections."

"Sounds great."

"Oh, and, uh, Jace?"

"Yeah?"

"I didn't see your name on the guest list for the party."

"I wasn't invited."

"Would you like to go?"

"I'm a party animal."

"Great." She didn't want to sound too excited so she took a breath before she spoke. "You're in."

"You're wonderful."

She blushed.

"Do you think that Piper will be there tonight?"

"I'm not sure," she said softly, her excitement replaced with disappointment.

"I heard Logan Barrister was back in town. That he was there at the hotel."

"No comment."

"Care to elaborate?"

"No, sorry."

"That's okay. Hey, I'll see you tonight."

"You bet. Bye." She hung up the phone. Would she never learn? She'd actually thought for a minute there, that they'd connected. A little, at least. It was silly, really. He was doing an article on Piper, what else would he want to talk about? Certainly not her. She wasn't anyone. Not anyone at all.

PIPER TURNED OFF the video camera. She wasn't at all sure she'd done the right thing. She could still just take the tape and leave. Trace would never know the difference.

She went into his bathroom, and sighed at her face.

Waterproof mascara. Great for swimming, lousy with tears. She pulled a tissue out and tried to fix the damage.

What was she hoping for here? That her from-the-heart confession would change things? Would have Trace whacking his forehead with a "Eureka, now I get it?" Wasn't going to happen. Trace believed a number of things about her, had believed those things for a long time. He had no reason to think she was telling him the truth. And even if he did buy that she was being completely frank, it probably wouldn't matter.

But she hoped it would.

She stared at herself in the mirror. "You like him," she said. "You like him more than you should. So what's up with that?"

Her reflection offered no theories. And it was almost time for their meeting with Kit.

Piper walked back into the bedroom, took the tape out of the machine and put it on his pillow. And promised herself she wasn't going to give it another thought. What he did with it was his business.

She gathered her things and left, making sure she had the key card to give back to the front desk. On her way to the elevator, she called Martin. "Where are you?" she asked, before he had a chance to speak.

"In the limo."

"Is Logan with you?"

"Yes, he is."

"Thank you."

"Can I ask you something?"

"Sure."

"Why? Last I heard, you guys were doing great."

"We were never doing great, Martin. In case you haven't noticed, your boy there is an alcoholic with a pretty bad drug problem. And FYI, he can't even get it up. So what we had was convenience. But it's no longer convenient, so do me a favor, and keep him close, okay? I don't want him at the party."

"Okay, Piper. I'll do that for you."

"And in return, you want…?"

"I'm not an alcoholic and I can still get it up."

She laughed. "Okay, Martin. You and a guest are on the list. Just make sure your guest isn't Logan."

"Deal."

She hung up. Wondering how on earth she could have thought that being seen with Logan could have ever appealed to her, even as a convenience. Actually, he was such a huge star, and such a wreck, she thought he might deflect a bit from her own ridiculous life.

Bad plan. Stupid plan.

Maybe the thing she had to do was drop out. Move to some remote island and just stay there until everyone forgot about her. Nice idea, bad timing. She had Hush now. And as much as she needed the hotel, Hush needed her right back. On the front page. But maybe, she could be on the front page fully clothed.

17

THE MEETING with Kit lasted three-and-a-half hours.
Trace sat in the conference room, staring at the new
drawings as Piper walked Kit out. He needed to process
everything that had happened.

Piper had been astonishing. She'd been more than ac-
commodating, and he figured if he brought the new
campaign to Nicholas, showed him the new direction,
Nicholas would back off. Well, he'd still want all the sex
accoutrements disposed of, but Trace didn't think that
was a deal breaker. Not after hearing Piper.

He stood and shuffled through the drawings that Kit
had come up with. She had some terrific ideas. They
needed to be fleshed out, finessed, but they pictured
Hush as a sophisticated place to stay, the only place to
stay if you wanted to be a player. They were still about
sex, just not overtly so. And Piper wasn't center stage.

He still hadn't shaken this afternoon. Not the way
Logan had looked at her, not the images that kept spinning in his head.

He wondered if Logan was still in her suite. And if
he was, was he staying?

The meeting had been all business, and with Kit there, he wasn't about to start anything personal. But now they were alone and he needed to get clear on some things.

"So what do you really think?"

He turned. Piper was standing at the door, arms crossed as she leaned against the frame. She was more beautiful than any woman he'd ever known. Of course he wanted her. And he doubted the ache would ever ease. "I think these are great. I'm impressed as hell."

"Kit's good."

"She is. But the credit, I think, belongs with you."

"I'm still not sure I'm going to go with them."

"What's the confusion? These are classy. Elegant. They're what the hotel is all about."

"*Also* what the hotel is about." She pushed off the door and came into the room. "I can't help but wonder what the media will make of the sudden shift. Will they think I've lost my nerve? That I no longer believe Hush is for lovers?"

"Maybe they'll just think this is a natural progression. That you're appealing to more than the libido."

"Perhaps. But I'd be willing to bet the first week's receipts that someone, somewhere, will find out that Nicholas had something to do with it."

"So what?"

She smiled. "Spoken as a man who's never been on the front page of *The Enquirer.*"

"They don't own you."

"Don't they?"

"Come on, Piper. You're stronger than that."

She gave him a look of utter astonishment.

"What?"

"You can say that to me? You?"

He stood up. Approached her, but when he got close, she backed away.

"I don't pretend to understand your life Piper, but I feel like I've gotten to know you a little better."

Her laughter was genuine. And insulting.

"Why is that so hard to believe?"

"You know what you read in the papers, Trace."

"What's going on, Piper? Why are you so angry?"

"I didn't invite Logan here. I had no idea he would show up."

"The press…"

"He brought them. His manager called, set it all up."

"So it wasn't planned."

"Not by me."

"Oh."

"Yeah. Oh. And thanks for asking." She walked around him, heading for the hallway.

"Hold on. Just wait."

She stopped, but she didn't turn around.

"Last I heard, you and Logan were an item."

Now she did turn, and looked at him with sadness. "I repeat. You know what you read in the papers."

"I don't know what to ask."

"What do you want to know?"

"Are you still seeing him?"

"No."

"Is there anyone else?"

She shook her head.

"Will you have dinner with me?"

"Not tonight."

"Fair enough."

"I have some calls to make."

He nodded, then watched her walk away. Before he left, he gathered all the papers together, put them in the portfolio. He'd planned on taking them to Nicholas in the morning, but maybe he'd hold off. Piper had said she wasn't sure and he didn't want to jump the gun.

He'd go to his room, have dinner. Call Piper later. He didn't want the conversation to end here. And he had the feeling she didn't, either.

"I THOUGHT YOU'D GONE."

Piper shook her head as she walked into Kit's office. It was just so Kit with her wee-smiley-face fetish. Everything from her clock to her screen saver had the big yellow grins, and every time Piper came into her office, her mood lifted.

"What's up?" Kit asked, pushing her long blond hair behind her shoulder.

"I want to set up a press conference. Tomorrow morning. Can we do it?"

"Sure. Want to give me a hint?"

"I'll talk about the new campaign, and I'm also going to announce that Logan and I are history."

"Uh, you sure you want to do that second part the morning of the party?"

"You think people are coming to see Logan or to see the hotel?"

"I don't think Logan's presence would be a bad thing."

"Well, he's not coming back here. Ever."

"It's your call."

"Tell me what you think of the new stuff, Kit. Bottom line."

"I think it's gorgeous. Classy."

"And?"

"I like things the way they are."

"Why?"

"You're kidding, right? The ad campaign is a wet dream. And I mean that on so many levels. Piper, sorry, but you're like one of the most famous women in the world. Why would I not want you in the ads? It doesn't hurt that you're totally hot, that the hotel is smokin', and you're going to be turning away anyone who's not on the A list."

"Now tell me what you really think."

"You asked."

"I know. But go ahead and put the conference together, okay? Early. We're going to need to clear the press out right after. Talk to Janice and see about getting the security team out first thing."

"Okay. Should I keep working on the designs?"

Piper nodded. "Thanks."

"No sweat, boss."

She left Kit's office and walked slowly toward her own. But she didn't want to go there, either.

Trace was probably in his room. And if he was in his room, he was watching the tape. Which made her really, really nervous.

She needed to do something to take her mind off things. Off him. She'd find Lisa. Lisa would help. Lisa always helped.

TRACE HADN'T MOVED a muscle since the tape started. He watched as Piper faced the camera unflinchingly, her voice soft and shaky, her eyes glistening with tears. His chest constricted as he listened to her naked honesty, at the pain that she'd hidden so well.

"My father immediately thought the worst," she said. "From the time I was in high school, and the paparazzi started getting nuts. He never asked me what really happened, or how they got the horrible pictures. He just figured I was exactly what they said I was. Even when I tried to explain, he'd look at me like I was lying."

Trace closed his eyes, unable to look at her, thinking about his own reactions to the media's portrait of Piper. Shame burned in his gut, and it was all he could do not to turn off the tape.

He'd looked at her torn blouse and immediately assumed she'd manipulated her own costume malfunction.

The truly sick thing was that he understood how the media worked. Especially the tabloids. They were held to no journalistic standards and they made things up as it suited them. So why had he even once entertained the idea that what they said about Piper was true?

He forced himself to watch her again. To listen.

"I admit, I gave up. I stopped fighting it, and I shouldn't have done that. It just felt so big. So I went with it. The men, the parties. I couldn't see another way.

Until school. Until Hush. And maybe I should have gone for something more tasteful, but dammit, there are some things I'm not ashamed of. I'm not the woman in the papers, but I am a sexual being. And the hell with anyone who wants to take that away from me.

"I don't want to lose my inheritance. But I don't want to lose myself, either." She laughed. "I'm just starting to really understand who that is. And now, I'm supposed to give it away."

There was more. The truth about her relationship with Logan. The circumstances behind some of her most infamous pictures. The time she went on the *Today* show to talk about a children's charity and the host had called her slutty twice. Nicely, of course, all in good fun. But it had hurt, and hurt deeply.

Finally, the tape ended, but not before the tears that had threatened spilled down her pale cheeks. Before her voice broke.

He turned off the machine. Then he sat back on the bed. He needed to think.

PIPER WORKED Amuse Bouche, stopping at several tables. There were a lot of celebrities tonight, all A list, and all invited to the opening-night party. She couldn't afford to miss a one, so it took her almost forty minutes to make it to Lisa's table.

She remembered the reporter but struggled a minute to recall his name. "Jace." She held out her hand, and he stood to greet her.

"You do that well," he said.

"I majored in Schmoozing 101."

"I'll bet you got an A plus."

She smiled at him, then turned to Lisa. "Hey."

Lisa nodded. "Sit down, Piper. We were just talking about you."

She sat, wondering what was up with her friend. Maybe Jace was being a jerk, which wouldn't surprise Piper in the least. She held no illusions about reporters. They appeared to be humans, but that was just a disguise. Inside they were sharks, always after their next prey.

"I was just wondering about you and Logan," Jace said. "Heard he was here."

"He's not," Piper said.

"But he was."

"That's right."

"And?"

"No and. He was here. He left."

"But what about you two? Is there trouble in paradise?"

She turned on him, struggling not to tell him what he could do with his incredibly lame questions. The man was writing a feature article for *Vanity Fair.* She could not afford to piss him off. "As much as I'd like to tell you, I can't. I will say that I'm having a press conference tomorrow, and I might mention something about Logan."

"No hints?"

She leaned over, eyeing him conspiratorially. "Here's a hint," she whispered. "The seared tuna is to die for."

At least it got a chuckle from Lisa. But underneath that, her friend was hurting, Piper could tell. They needed to talk, but it wasn't going to happen yet. Piper got up, put her hand on Lisa's shoulder. "Call me later, okay?"

"Sure."

"Nice seeing you again, Jace. Please be nice to Lisa. She's very important."

He didn't even look at Lisa. Not even a glance.

Piper didn't get it. Her best friend was incredible. Beautiful, smart, funny. Men were so stupid sometimes.

She worked the room one more time, suddenly so tired she felt she could fall asleep on her feet. On the plus side, she hadn't thought about Trace for, what, ten minutes? That was something.

Once she was in the lobby, she checked to make sure everything was in good shape, spoke to Elliot, the concierge on duty, and that was it. She went to the elevator, too exhausted to even stop and visit Eartha Kitty.

The ride up seemed long, and the walk to her suite even longer. But finally, she was inside. She didn't even turn on the light as she headed for the bedroom.

Somehow, she wasn't surprised to see Trace waiting for her in the darkened room. Just glad. Really, really glad.

LISA GOT OUT of the elevator on the roof. The garden lights were lit, and she realized this might be one of the last times she could ever come up here with the expectation of having it to herself.

It was her favorite part of the hotel. She loved coming up here any time, but late at night was her favorite. The lights of Manhattan were a picture-perfect backdrop to the solitude. Even with the sun long set the scent of the flowers made her think of spring days. Come to think of it, she hadn't seen much of spring. The hotel had eaten up her days. Her life.

She walked over to the swing, sat down. She was twenty-eight and she was head of human resources for a major hotel. She was appreciated for her efforts, very well paid, had the best colleagues in the world. Her life was privileged in a hundred ways, not the least of which was access to the most important and influential people of her time.

And she was sitting in a swing bemoaning the fact that she didn't have a date. What's wrong with this picture?

She might be living in Piper's shadow, but it was a choice, not a prison. She could leave anytime, but she didn't. Why? Because living in Piper's shadow was an awesome experience. In fact, it was a hell of a lot easier than being the woman herself.

Piper was enviably strong, and what she'd done was nothing short of miraculous, all things considered. Her father considered. And if it was hard for Lisa to find someone special, it had been damn near impossible for Piper.

Except, something was going on with Trace, and Lisa hoped like hell the two of them could get past their history. He was good for her. He didn't roll over, let her get her way at every turn. Men either wanted to be cavemen with her or puppy dogs. Trace was strong and decent. The biggest problem Lisa could see was his job. How could they possibly have a relationship if he continued to work for Nicholas Devon? Couldn't happen.

Wait, maybe it could. Maybe a lot of things could happen. Hush was here, right? And it was going to be a massive success. And she was living out her dream job.

She smiled. Why was it always so easy to focus on the negative, even when there were a hundred positives all around her? And why on earth was she so upset about not getting Jace? He was nice-looking, but he was severely lacking a sense of humor, and eek, why would she want that?

The next second it hit her. Here she was a single woman living in the sexiest hotel on earth, and she hadn't done one thing about it. Well, that wasn't exactly true, she had used one of the personal toys in her room, but as far as the true spirit of Hush, she was a sham. A mockery. She should be ashamed of herself.

She wasn't living *la vida loca*. She was living *la vida* loser.

No more. From now on, she would take her pleasures where she found them, and let the chips fall where they may. She may not find true love, but she could certainly find the perfect orgasm.

Breathing deeply, she turned to look at the city lights. If she wasn't tone deaf, she'd break out in song. Instead, she did a little happy dance. Really glad no one was there to see her but the moon.

"SODA'S FINE," Trace said.

Piper stood at the bar, deciding that she wasn't nearly as noble as Trace and that she needed something stronger. It took her a few minutes to finish putting their drinks together, but that's because her hands weren't particularly steady.

Trace wanted to talk. He'd seen her tape, of course. She'd wanted this. It's why she'd made the tape in the first place. To set things straight between them, put all their cards on the table. And now that it was here, she was scared to death.

She brought the drinks, putting his next to him on the table by the couch. She sat across from him, wanting to see his face clearly. "So," she said.

Trace took a deep breath as he studied her face. She couldn't ever remember being looked at like that. As if he could see something no one else could. "I sat for a long time after I turned off the machine," he said. "It was a lot to take in."

"My life and times."

He nodded. "I know 'I'm sorry' is inadequate. That it makes up for nothing."

"No. It helps."

"I should have looked deeper."

"You had no reason to. I was just your boss's daughter. No biggie."

"That's not true. If it was, you think we would have fought like we did? I always liked you, Piper. What I knew of you. It was the image I had difficulty with, and now I see that it wasn't even yours."

"That's a nice thought, but it's not accurate. It wasn't mine to begin with, but it became mine. You weren't wrong."

He leaned forward, put his elbows on his knees. The

intensity of his gaze held her motionless. "I was wrong. On some very fundamental levels. Not because I'm stupid, but because I'm lazy. It was easier. The path of least resistance. When it comes to working for Nicholas, I've always done that. It's not something I'm proud of."

"I remember when you used to talk about doing something else."

He nodded. "I gave up those dreams a long time ago. Didn't think much about it until this week."

"What do you mean?"

He wiped his face with the palm of his hand, then he looked away, at the window. "I had a friend in college, Bob Steiner. Great guy, hell of a chess player. We were close. Real close. He went on to work for his family's company, clothing manufacturers out of New Jersey. I went to work for my family. Well, your family. We kept in touch, but as time went on we didn't see each other that often.

"Two nights after your seventeenth birthday, Bob called me. He was in trouble. He didn't say what, he just said he needed me. To represent him in a legal matter. I could tell he wasn't kidding, that he was into something serious. But Nicholas wanted me to go to England, to finish up the contracts on the Devon hotel in Hyde Park. I gave Bob the name of a lawyer I knew. Told him I'd call when I got back."

"What happened?"

"I wrapped it up in England. Took a few days for myself in Wales. I had a great time. The weather was perfect."

She didn't press him, but she wished he'd look at her. He just kept staring out the window. Finally, his head dipped.

"When I came back I found out Bob had been indicted for embezzlement. But it never went to court. He hung himself."

"Oh, God."

"Did I mention how great the weather was in Wales?"

18

"YOU DIDN'T KILL HIM."

Trace looked at her, finally. His face was flushed and his lips were tight. "I didn't help."

"So you think you should have told your father and mine to stuff it? Quit when you were just starting out?"

"I could have done a lot of things. That's just one of them."

She went over to the couch, needing to touch more than she needed to see. Her hand went over his. "You couldn't have known."

He smiled at her. "I think you're an amazing woman. And I think your hotel is just as amazing."

"Thank you."

"The whole reason I told you my sad tale is because I know from experience that we have to sleep in the beds we make for a long time."

"What do you want, Trace? I used to know your dreams, but I have no idea what they are now."

"I don't have any."

"Everyone has dreams."

"No."

"Everything in your life is perfect? Just the way you want it?"

He shook his head. Turned his hand and threaded his fingers through hers. "It's looking up."

"I made the tape so that we could start again. But we can't do that if you're not willing to really talk to me."

"What have I been doing?"

"Okay, you're making headway, but this dream thing— I don't buy it. I think there are lots of things you want in your life."

"Like?"

"More in-line skating. Fewer meetings you could do in your sleep."

"I see."

"Making a difference."

"You don't think running the Devon empire makes a difference?"

"I think you could do anything you wanted to. Your own practice, maybe doing some pro bono work on the side. You're a smart guy. I just think it would be great if you were a happy guy, too."

"Are you?"

"A happy guy?"

"Scratch the last part."

"Sometimes," she said. "Hush makes me happy. I really needed to do something with myself. Something I felt deeply about. That mattered."

"And you are."

"It shouldn't matter. Giving rich people a nice place to screw."

"If I thought that's all this was, I would have been out of here day two."

"Honest?"

He nodded. "It took me a while, but I get it now. This is a special place. You make it special."

She touched the side of his face. She loved the feel of his skin. The look in his eyes. "I'm happy right now," she said.

He nodded just before he leaned in and touched his lips to hers. So gently. She sighed into his mouth, welcoming his breath in return. They'd passed through something, although she wasn't sure what. A moment, a truth. For the first time they were both here in the same space. Not in their respective corners.

His hand went to the back of her head, holding her steady as the kiss deepened. The moist tip of his tongue slipped between her lips and she opened to him. He moved closer to her, tilting his head toward perfect. They moved together, a synchrony from somewhere deep, a click, a slide, a fit.

They stood together, parting, but he didn't let go of her hand. They walked together to the bedroom, and it was so different.

They took each other's clothes off, slowly, piece by piece. She rubbed her hands over his shirt, feeling the heat of his skin beneath. She opened the buttons easily, spreading the material to reveal the soft, dark hair on his chest. Not much, mostly in the center. She kissed him there as she continued to undress him, breathing in his scent. His nipples had hardened and she moved to the right, swirling her tongue. His gasp went straight through her as she lifted her arms so he could remove her blouse.

The pace quickened as she went to his belt. He unzipped her skirt. He pushed down as she did, both of them taking their underwear along for the ride.

She let him take off her thigh-highs, shoes and bra. The clothes stayed on the floor while they climbed into bed, under the covers.

Close together, touching everything, everywhere, they found each other's mouths. There wasn't any urgency, the need to prove a thing. It was utterly unlike the sex they'd had before. She felt as if she needed to learn him all over again.

Long, slow strokes of his hand down her back, her side. The brush of his knuckles across her belly, making her writhe against him. His hard length fitting between her thighs.

He pulled back. "Stay right here," he whispered. Then he reached over the bed to grab a condom. She didn't waste the opportunity. She touched him, rubbing his cock with her palm just to feel his flesh. To hear his low moan.

Then his hand was on hers, and she let him go. His hot breath warmed her neck, and his fingers slipped inside her. She was ready. And she wanted nothing more than to feel him.

"Now," she whispered.

He nodded, moved over her, careful to balance his weight on his arms. Moving slowly, he entered her, and as he filled her, she cried out from the sweetness of it.

Once he was all the way inside, he stilled. She curled her legs around his thighs. No acrobatics, no artifice. Just…them.

"I've always wanted to make love to you," he said, his face inches from her own, their gazes locked.

"Me, too. Since I was seventeen," she said.

"It was worth the wait."

She nodded. "Every minute."

And then he began to move, those same languid strokes. They kissed, deep and slow. She didn't even notice she was crying until she felt a tear trickle down her cheek.

HE WOKE when the phone rang. Piper groaned as she picked up the line, and he kissed the center of her back before he headed to the bathroom. There had been a number of calls last night, up until midnight or so. The party preparations were in full swing all over the hotel. Construction, decorations, music, food. It was a madhouse down there. Thank goodness Piper had the staff to handle everything but the biggest issues. By the time he returned, she was slipping on her robe. "What's wrong?" he asked.

"That was my father. He wants to see me. Now."

"I'll be ready in ten."

"No, Trace. Thank you, but I need to see him alone."

"What are you going to do?"

She studied him for a long minute. "I don't know."

He rounded the bed and took her in his arms. "You'll do the right thing."

She smiled. "I wish I knew what that was."

"You do."

"Oh?"

"Trust yourself. I do."

"So if I tell him I'm not changing a thing?"

"I've been thinking about that. He'll cut you out of the will. There's nothing you're going to say to him that will convince him to do otherwise. He's stubborn, and he thinks he's right."

"What do you think?"

"I already told you. I trust you."

"That's not answering the question."

He kissed her. "I'll be here when you get back."

She touched his face. "Wow, huh?"

"Yeah, wow."

"How about conserving some water?"

"Sounds good."

She led him across the room, but stopped just short of the bathroom door. "Press conference."

"What?"

"I have to make a call." She went back to the bed, got her phone and pressed the buttons. He grabbed his boxers from the floor and slipped them on, not sure if he should wait.

"Dad, it's me. I can't see you now. I have a press conference this morning. If you want to talk, you'll need to come here."

Trace froze. Watching her expression, he knew Nicholas was not happy. No big surprise. Mohammed didn't like coming off the mountain, not for anything as trivial as his only daughter. Bastard.

"Okay, well, I'll call you when I'm done." Piper turned off her phone, then turned to him, giving him a tight smile. "Let's do that whole shower thing, shall we?"

"I'll wash your back…"

She took him by the hand and didn't let him go until it was time to grab the soap.

"PIPER, WHAT'S GOING ON with you and Logan?"

"Is Logan going to be at the party?"

"There have been reports that both Britney and Christina are coming to the party, is that true?"

Piper held up her hand and moved closer to the microphones. "Okay, first things first. Logan Barrister will not be coming to the party. He will not be coming to Hush at all, as far as I know."

The flashbulbs went off like strobe lights in a disco. Piper waited, giving them a chance to scribble and point. When the first wave of reaction ebbed, she made sure her smile was nicely in place. "If you have further questions about Logan, I suggest you get in touch with him."

"Did he sleep with someone else, Piper?"

"Did you sleep with someone else?"

Piper held her hand up. "End of discussion. Now, the other reason I asked you here is to talk about tonight's party. We're setting up a red carpet outside the hotel. You can liaise with Janice Foster and Lisa Scott to find out about accessibility and I'm sure all of you will get lots and lots of great photos and stories, but you're not getting them inside Hush. This is a private party, invitation only, and we're not giving an inch."

A collective groan made her grin bigger.

"I know you'll all survive, and if you play nicely, we'll make sure that all the biggies come in the front entrance."

"Do you have a list?"

"Yes, but it's as private as the party."

"Piper? I heard a rumor that your father is insisting that you change the image of the hotel. That he wants you to change the ads and take out all the sex."

She recognized the reporter asking the question. Her name was Holly Wilson, and she worked for the *Post*. She was a beautiful older woman who often accompanied Piper's father to social events. There was no doubt that her "rumor" had come right from the horse's mouth. Nicholas had worked fast. It hadn't even been two hours since their phone conversation.

"Piper?"

She looked beyond the reporters, searching near the walls until she found Trace. He looked incredibly dashing and elegant, and that was just his eyes. "Nothing about Hush is going to change," she said, keeping her gaze on Trace. Her stomach tightened as she realized that little sentence was worth a half-a-billion dollars. "This is not a Devon hotel. It's Hush, and it will continue to be Hush, and no one and nothing is going to change that."

And still, she looked at Trace. There was such trust and encouragement in his expression that she kept her mouth shut, even though a very large part of her wanted to take it all back.

There were more questions, all shouted rapid-fire,

but she'd said what she needed to. Everything was out there. The hotel would make her or break her, but it would be hers. No one else's.

For the first time in years, she felt herself tremble in front of the cameras. Because it was a new Piper talking. She might be a Devon but she was her own woman now.

She found Trace again and he turned his head, inviting her to follow his gaze. "Oh, shit," she whispered, as she saw Nicholas Devon's secretary standing by the door. She didn't look happy. Marilyn put her cell phone to her ear, turned and slipped out the door.

Piper wondered if her father would ever speak to her again. If he still even thought of her as his daughter. The room dimmed and she had to grab hold of the podium to steady herself.

She knew she should be responding to the questions, but she couldn't. The reality of what she'd done kept getting larger and larger, and along with it her fear.

And then she felt a hand on her shoulder. She looked up to see Trace, standing right behind her. He shifted until he was closer to the microphones.

"Thank you, ladies and gentlemen. That's it. I'm sure we'll see all of you tonight on the red carpet. Remember to see Janice Foster or Lisa Scott if you have any questions."

His hand went around her waist, and he led her off the podium. She leaned on him, took comfort in his strong arms. A few minutes later, they were alone in the elevator. He put his card key in for the roof.

She rested her head against his shoulder. He hugged

her close, all the way to the top. Once they were out-side, standing in the garden, the scent of April thick and sweet, he touched her chin with his finger, lifting her head so he could meet her gaze. "You did it."

She nodded. "I think I'm going to throw up."

"Sounds reasonable."

She laughed. "You do realize what I've given up?"

He nodded. "I also realize what you've gained."

"A hotel."

"Your soul and your hotel. It's going to be sensational."

"I sure hope so. I'm ridiculously spoiled."

"I know."

"And there are lots of people depending on me."

"I know that, too."

"And still, you're here."

He smiled. "Actually, I just came up to hit you up for a job."

"Oh?"

"Yeah. I'm not really a Devon kind of lawyer any-more. It's my obsession with sex. It's not at all digni-fied. Frankly, I disgrace the name."

"Sex, huh?"

"You know me. A firm believer in exploring all things sensual. Hell, I keep a copy of the *Kama Sutra* in my night-table drawer."

Piper pinched his butt. In a good way. "A hotel like this needs a good attorney."

"That's what I was thinking."

"And now that I'm not under my father's auspices, I'll need someone to handle my personal affairs."

"Uh-huh."

"So maybe we can work something out."

"First, I need to go talk to my father," he said. "And then I'll be heading over to the Orpheus."

"That's not going to be pretty."

He kissed her. "I'll be back in plenty of time for tonight's festivities."

"Okay."

Then he kissed her again. When he finally pulled back, he gave her the oddest look.

"What?"

"It's been one hell of a week."

"I'll say."

"It's as if we've just met."

"New beginnings all over the damn place."

He laughed. She wasn't quite at the laughing stage, but when she smiled, it was real. It felt good.

19

IT WAS SEVEN, and the hotel was ready. The party was outrageously large, spanning the entire property. Piper had no doubt that by the time the evening was over, her guests would be hooked. So many were spending the night that they were sold out, and she knew after this that the bookings would go through the roof.

She checked herself one more time in the mirror, blessing Donatella Versace for the fabulous red gown. It was simple, but perfect. She'd had Sam Fine come in to do her makeup, and he'd outdone himself. She was happy; still reeling from her decision, but deep down, she knew she'd done the right thing.

Now, all she needed was Trace.

She could still hardly believe what had happened with him. It had all begun so many years ago, and while she blushed when she thought about what she'd done on her seventeenth birthday, it seemed like something of a miracle that they'd come to this. What this was, exactly, wasn't clear, but it was good. That much she knew for sure.

She headed to the elevator, amazed that she could

walk so comfortably in her ridiculously high Jimmy Choos. There were three stops on the way down, on the tenth, fifth and fourth floors. She didn't know the people, but they obviously knew who she was, because there were the traditional covert stares. Piper welcomed the guests, and wished them a good time. That seemed adequate, and it made her forget about what she was about to face.

She remembered when they hit the lobby.

The party wasn't really supposed to start until nine, yet the lobby was packed. Everyone looked like they were going to the MTV Video Music Awards, dressed to the nines with enough bling-bling to give Tiffany's a run for their money.

She should talk. The necklace she wore was worth a quarter of a million. A legacy from her mother, one she loved beyond words. Her fingers went to the diamonds and their cool reassurance.

Taking a deep breath, she walked into the night of her life. Waiters with trays passed champagne in the lobby, all of them looking fabulous in their black tuxes with pink ties, and of course, the pink Hush logos. Piper smiled and chatted, working it as she headed to her first stop, Erotique.

The bar was about a quarter full, but she'd wager in an hour it would be S.R.O. Champagne flowed, but most of the folks in here were ordering cocktails. The band, an extraordinary local group Eddie had discovered, was finishing their setup. She'd asked them to start at eight. Although she wanted vodka, she made her way to the bar and ordered a soda with four cherries. It might be the only food she'd get all night.

Kelly Preston came over to say hi, letting Piper know that hubby John Travolta was nearby. Piper had done a fund-raiser with the couple, and it was a nice catch-up. But then Kelly moved on, and Piper needed her soda.

"Can I get that drink for you?"

She spun around. "Oh," she said, looking up at Trace. "How did it go?"

He smiled. "I'll tell you all about it later. What's far more important at the moment is that you look sensational."

"Trace."

"Please."

She sighed. Then she looked him over. A black Armani tux with a dark-silver silk shirt and tie. "Oh, honey," she said. "I think you're gonna get so lucky tonight."

"Thank God," he said.

He kissed her to the accompaniment of a flashbulb. She tried to catch the miscreant, but there were too many people milling about. It was inevitable that people would sneak in cameras. Especially now when they came in such tiny packages. She couldn't very well have everyone frisked.

"It doesn't matter." Trace kissed her again. "What are you having?"

"Cherries, with some soda thrown in."

"You wild woman."

"Don't mess with me."

He caught the attention of the bartender and ordered himself a Stoli. "The place looks fabulous."

"Everyone's worked their butts off. I've been assured that it will all run like clockwork. However, I'm still reserving the right to throw up."

"Good plan." He got his drink and hers. "Shall we go explore?"

"We shall."

He wrapped his arm around her waist and led her through the growing crowd.

Back in the lobby, she found Janice, who despite the fact that she hadn't slept for about twenty hours, still looked wonderful.

"Well?"

"The mob outside is being abnormally well behaved, so I called in for reinforcements."

Piper laughed. "Excellent, Janice. What about the limos?"

"Not a problem. The NYPD is being very cooperative. Probably because the mayor is going to be here in twenty, but I'll take what I can get."

"Super. Where's Lisa?"

"Last I saw, she was in Exhibit A."

"Thanks. Give me a holler if you need me. I've got my cell."

"Great." She turned in her pretty black dress and headed for the exit. Piper saw Mick in his tux waiting for her at the door.

"Let's do Amuse before we head down, okay?"

"Food?"

"Yes. Food. If it's set out. If not, we'll sneak into the kitchen."

It took a while to go the short distance to the restaurant. Lots of people to schmooze, lots of cheeks to kiss. Lots and lots of celebrities. Everyone from Larry King to Beyoncé. When they finally reached the restaurant, she saw that Chef had outdone himself. The hors d'oeuvres were out of this world, with delicacies like poached oysters garnished with osetra caviar and vermouth sauce, warm quail salad, boudin of lobster, shrimp and scallops with sofrito and Nantua sauce, and many other scrumptious goodies.

Trace made himself a small plate, but she was happy with her cherries. More and more people wanted to talk to her, everyone declaring their undying allegiance to Hush and promising to stay forever, but now that the worst of her jitters were over, she wanted to get Trace alone and find out what had happened with his father and hers.

It didn't work out that way. The mayor showed up, and that was an event in itself. He was very nice, but she could tell he was sorry the press hadn't been allowed inside. Janice quietly assured her he'd been properly treated by the hordes, and that he was simply still basking in the glow.

She made nice, he made politics to everyone within earshot, and by the time she was through, they needed her in Exhibit A.

Trace stayed by her the whole time, which was the most incredible feeling. It was amazing to have him at her back. He wouldn't let her fall. He wouldn't even let her trip. He was simply there, her own personal rock.

That made her think naughty things, which she couldn't possibly act upon now, so instead, she stole a kiss on their way down to the sofa bar.

It was Eddie who'd paged, and she understood when she walked into the bar. Something was wrong with the sound system. Before she could panic, Trace took her by the shoulders, asked who was in charge, and told her he'd handle it. Boom, just like that, she relaxed. There was no doubt that he'd do whatever it took to make it right, and she didn't have to do a thing but walk around and compliment movie stars on their wardrobe choices.

She began with Halle Berry, who was devastatingly stunning, and moved on to Edie Falco. Good lord, there were more stars than in the heavens: Matthew and Sara Jessica, Jude Law and Sienna Miller. Even Dash Black. Insanity. But great insanity.

The best thing of all though, was when she saw Lisa. She looked glorious. Not just because of her Valentino gown, which was beyond the beyond, but because she looked the happiest Piper had ever seen her. Smiling like a coquette, she was deep into major flirting with the terminally adorable George Clooney, and from this angle, Mr. Clooney didn't stand a chance.

The sound of jazz filled the room. Not just one speaker, but all of them, from below and above and all sides. They'd hired one of the best quartets in the world, and in the first few bars they'd earned their fee.

She looked around for Trace, admiring the dancers as they spun through the room, the blue lights skimming the walls, making the guests look fabulously exotic.

As she caught sight of Trace, her spirits soared even higher. She felt like the queen of New York, and she knew, without a doubt, that she'd made the right decision. But there were still things to do.

Not with the hotel. With that gorgeous guy smiling as he made his way to her. He never even looked at the world-class women all around him. Just her.

"All better," he said.

She put her hand over his heart. "Perfect."

"Do you need to be in this room?"

She shook her head.

"How about a visit to the garden?"

"You bet."

Half an hour later, they were on the rooftop. Not alone, unfortunately, but it wasn't crowded, and they were able to scope out a private corner. It was so beautiful. All the bowers and arbors twinkled with sparkly white lights. The flowers smelled divine, and the only music was the trickle of the fountains.

Trace found a nice bench, then pulled her down next to him. "You throw a great party."

"Thanks. I had help."

"We all need help from time to time."

"Speaking of which, what happened?"

"It was better and worse."

"Than?"

"Better than being stung by millions of wasps, worse than getting the Nobel Peace Prize."

She laughed. "Anyone ever tell you that when you're not being a stuffy prick, you're very, very cute?"

"No."

"It's true. Now tell me."

"Well, Dad was reasonably cool. After he finished about a half hour of telling me what a schmuck I was, and how I could have permanently destroyed his entire life, he said if I wanted to stay with the firm, I could, but only if Nicholas didn't fire everyone."

"Cool."

"I thought so."

She grabbed his hand. "What about Nicholas?"

"He's a troubled man."

She laughed again. "Tell me something I don't know."

"He's having an affair with the reporter from the *Post.*"

"Trace."

"Okay. He tried to give me a great deal of money to convince you to change your mind."

"Did you take it?"

"Oh, yeah. I already ordered my yacht. I'm calling it the *Irredeemable Bastard.*"

"Sweet."

"I also informed him that I was now the official counsel for Hush and Piper Devon. He, uh, tried to convince me that he could take the hotel, that it was his money that built it, but I reminded him that I'd been the one to draw up the papers on the trust and that he had no claim whatsoever. Contracts were pulled. Things were said. Frankly, I didn't even know your father knew those words, but eventually, he conceded."

"Wow. I guess that means we shouldn't invite him for dinner next week, huh."

Trace's face lost its humor. "No, honey. I'm not saying you two will never reconcile, but it's gonna be a while. A long while."

"Did you see Kyle?"

He smiled again. "Yeah. He told me to tell you 'Way to go.'"

"I'll bet he was already celebrating. He's now the only child he's always wanted to be."

"On the other hand, you have made this hotel. You've built something real. Yours. No one else in the world could have done it. Just you. I hope you're not upset that I plan to ride on your coattails."

She swallowed hard. "Yeah?"

He nodded. "There's one more thing I thought I'd better mention."

"What's that?"

He brought her hand to his lips and kissed her gently. "I've kind of fallen in love with you."

Piper's whole body shivered. No words, nothing in her life had ever felt like this. "Oh," she whispered.

He winced. "That's it? Oh?"

She looked at him through her lashes. "Oh, goody?"

"Better," he said.

Leaning in, she kissed him. A real doozy. A kiss that told him she'd kinda fallen in love with him, too. That they were beginning anew, that they were beginning together. That whatever happened, they'd be fine. Really fine.

He kissed her back. His hands pulled her tight, and she melted against him. Tongues and teeth and sighs. A joy that blocked out the rest of the world.

It was only the lack of oxygen that made them part. She blinked back tears as she looked at him. "I love you," she said. "Always have. I just forgot for a little while."

"That's good to know," he said.

"You don't think they'd miss me if we left, do you?"

He laughed. "Uh, yeah. Sadly, I do. But tell you what. After midnight, they're on their own. It'll be just you and me."

"It's a deal."

He kissed her again, then pulled her up to stand next to him. "Let's go knock 'em dead, shall we?"

She nodded. "Just stay close, okay?"

He squeezed her hand. "Always."

Get ready to check-in to the Hush Hotel
in June 2005 with THRILL ME
by Isabel Sharpe.
Here's a sneak preview...

MEMORANDUM
To: Staff
From: Janice Foster, General Manager, HUSH Hotel
Date: Sunday
Re: Trevor Little

Mr. Trevor Little will be bringing another guest this week. We will be following the usual pattern of gifts: flowers Monday, spa visit Tuesday, bracelet Wednesday, negligee Thursday and the molded chocolate Friday. Reminder to treat his guest with absolute courtesy and not to act as if you've seen him here before. As usual, calls to his room should be forwarded to his voice mail automatically, and anyone asking for him should be told he is not registered here.

Note on housekeeping board:
Someone else gets to clean Trevor Little's room. I got it last time. Yick!

IF SHE THOUGHT of the Midwest Airlines airplane as a womb, and the jetway into Newark airport as a birth canal, then May Hope Ellison figured she was about to be reborn. Her first symbolic breaths of new life were only yards away, in the hallowed area outside gate B40.

Okay, maybe that was pushing it.

She'd been planning to fly into LaGuardia, after all Manhattan was her destination, but Trevor had insisted she fly into Newark. Save her the traffic and hassle of LaGuardia. And with luck, he'd get out of his meeting in New Jersey early and be able to meet her on the eleven-thirty-five train.

May's mother, born and bred in Wisconsin, but had lived in the Big Apple for a year or two of her premarital days, had shrugged and said she never had any trouble at LaGuardia.

Of course May hadn't told her mother about Trevor. Mothers didn't generally get very excited about daughters flying halfway across the country to spend a week of wild passion in a luxury boutique hotel with a man they barely knew.

Well, maybe they did get excited. But not in a good way.

One more step, around the corner, her first sight of her new temporary life and—wow. Lots of gates. Lots of noise. Lot and lots of people. This was not Milwaukee. And it certainly wasn't Oshkosh.

May wasn't aware she'd stopped dead until someone bumped into her and muttered something not terribly flattering or polite.

Forward, then, going with the flow, heading out of the gate-studded cul-de-sac, up a long corridor, then around another corner into the main terminal. Even more people. She clutched the directions Trevor had e-mailed her and followed signs for the shuttle to the NJ Transit train that would take her into the city.

After much confusion, buying the wrong ticket to the wrong destination—why would they name both the New York and New Jersey stations Penn Station?—she made it onto the right train, counting the cars carefully so she'd be in the one she and Trevor agreed upon. Third behind the engine.

Unfortunately, he wasn't there. Or fortunately, depending on whose nerves you asked. Not that she wasn't thrilled to be doing this, of course she was. It's just that…well how did you behave during a long commute with someone you barely knew that you were planning to screw for an entire week?

Hey, how are you? Hot for this time of year, isn't it? Looking forward to penetrating me?

Maybe it was better they'd meet at the hotel.

Half an hour later, May emerged from the train onto a hot, dark, underground platform, dragging her rolling suitcase behind her. She inched along, in closer proximity to more strangers than she cared to be, and struggled up the stairs into Penn Station.

Onward to her adventure. She'd met Trevor a month ago when he'd come through for the University of Wisconsin "spirit day" celebration and stopped by to catch up with an old professor at the business school, where she worked as assistant to the Dean.

They'd hit it off immediately. Gone from polite chat, to his invitation for coffee, to his invitation to drinks, to his invitation to dinner, to his invitation to his hotel room, which she'd declined, though she'd been tempted. When had any man paid this much attention to her? Then after he left town, he'd e-mailed her. Called her. And, incredibly, called her again. Until chatting with him became a part of her day she looked forward to. A bright spot in the last few dismal months since Dan had pronounced their six-year relationship over, because he wasn't feeling the excitement anymore.

Of course she couldn't stop him going where he needed to go. But feeling left behind sucked, not to mention feeling as if your guts had been ripped out. Though she knew Dan top to bottom, and couldn't help the sneaking feeling that after he sowed whatever oats he felt he had to sow, he'd be back and their lives would progress smoothly toward eternity as they'd always planned. Life was beautiful and miraculous all on its own. You didn't need to keep creating adrenaline rushes to enjoy it.

Okay, so she was after one now. Probably in reaction to what Dan had said about her, about their lives together. Dull and predictable? Not this week, honey. The e-mails and phone calls with Trevor had gotten increasingly intimate. Increasingly…sexual in tone. Why not? Dan was the only man she'd ever been with, and she was admittedly curious. Trevor was extremely attractive, and he must be a gazillionaire because he'd unexpectedly and thrillingly invited her to stay with him for a week at Hush Hotel in Manhattan.

If you enjoyed what you just read,
then we've got an offer you can't resist!

Take 2 bestselling love stories FREE!

Plus get a FREE surprise gift!

Clip this page and mail it to Harlequin Reader Service®

IN U.S.A.	**IN CANADA**
3010 Walden Ave.	P.O. Box 609
P.O. Box 1867	Fort Erie, Ontario
Buffalo, N.Y. 14240-1867	L2A 5X3

YES! Please send me 2 free Blaze™ novels and my free surprise gift. After receiving them, if I don't wish to receive anymore, I can return the shipping statement marked cancel. If I don't cancel, I will receive 4 brand-new novels each month, before they're available in stores! In the U.S.A., bill me at the bargain price of $3.99 plus 25¢ shipping and handling per book and applicable sales tax, if any*. In Canada, bill me at the bargain price of $4.47 plus 25¢ shipping and handling per book and applicable taxes**. That's the complete price and a savings of at least 10% off the cover prices—what a great deal! I understand that accepting the 2 free books and gift places me under no obligation ever to buy any books. I can always return a shipment and cancel at any time. Even if I never buy another book from Harlequin, the 2 free books and gift are mine to keep forever.

150 HDN DZ9K
350 HDN DZ9L

Name	(PLEASE PRINT)	
Address	Apt.#	
City	State/Prov.	Zip/Postal Code

Not valid to current Harlequin Blaze™ subscribers.

Want to try two free books from another series?
Call 1-800-873-8635 or visit www.morefreebooks.com.

* Terms and prices subject to change without notice. Sales tax applicable in N.Y.
** Canadian residents will be charged applicable provincial taxes and GST.
 All orders subject to approval. Offer limited to one per household.
® and ™ are registered trademarks owned and used by the trademark owner and or its licensee.

BLZ04R   ©2004 Harlequin Enterprises Limited.

Enjoy the launch of Maureen Child's NEW miniseries

THREE-WAY WAGER

The Reilly triplets bet they could go ninety days without sex. Hmmm.

The Tempting Mrs. Reilly
by MAUREEN CHILD

(Silhouette Desire #1652)
Available May 2005

Brian Reilly had just made a bet to not have sex for three months when his stunningly sexy ex-wife blew into town. It wasn't long before Tina had him contemplating giving up his wager and getting her back. But the tempting Mrs. Reilly had a reason of her own for wanting Brian to lose his bet... to give her a baby!

HARLEQUIN® *Blaze*™

The streets of New Orleans
are heating up with

BIG EASY
Bad Boys

Jeanie London

brings us an entire family of men with charm
and good looks to spare! You won't want
to miss Anthony DiLeo's story in

UNDER HIS SKIN
Harlequin Blaze #181
May 2005

Anthony is about to find out how an indecent proposal
fits into a simple business plan. When he approaches
Tess Hardaway with an idea to benefit both their companies,
she counters with an unexpected suggestion. A proposition
that involves the two of them getting to know each other
in the most intimate way!

Look for this book at your favorite retail outlet.